MIDSUMMER CENTURY

Never before had he even dreamed it possible that a man could be thrown out of his own mind by someone else – and this was not even his own mind; here, he was the interloper. There seemed to be no way to resist, nothing that he could even grab hold of – even had he been inhabiting his own brain, he would have known no better that any other man of his time in what part of it his psyche resided. Qvant knew, that was evident, and was homing upon it with the mercilessness of a guided missile . . .

James Blish

MIDSUMMER CENTURY

ARROW BOOKS

ARROW BOOKS LTD
3 Fitzroy Square, London W1

An imprint of the Hutchinson Publishing Group

London Melbourne Sydney Auckland
Wellington Johannesburg Cape Town
and agencies throughout the world

First published in England in 1973
Arrow edition 1975

*Made and printed in Great Britain
by Hunt Barnard Printing Ltd., Aylesbury, Bucks*

ISBN 0 09 909720 6

To George Hay

NOTE

I am indebted to Rowland Bowen and Dr. John Clark, both of England, for substantial elements of my hypotheses about the nature of ESP and mystical experience, respectively. In both instances I have simply helped myself to whatever seemed useful in advancing my own notions, and my story, without trying to be rigorous about it. The theories remain their intellectual properties and await their own expositions of them. I am grateful to both for permission to simplify their work into fiction.

JAMES BLISH

Harpsden (Henley)
Oxon, England
1971

PART ONE
REBIRTH III

In all the ointment which the world had provided for the anointing of John Martels, D.Sc., F.R.A.S., etc., there was only one fly: There was something wrong with his telescope.

Martels, unmarried and 30, was both a statistic and a beneficiary of what his British compatriots were bitterly calling the brain-drain, the luring of the best English minds to the United States with higher pay, lower taxes, and the apparent absence of any class system whatsoever. And he had found no reason to regret it, let alone feel guilty about it. Both his parents were dead, and as far as he was concerned, he owed the United Kingdom nothing any more.

Of course, the advantages of living in the States were not quite so unclouded as they had been presented to him, but he had never expected anything else. Take the apparent absence of a class system, for instance: All the world knew that the blacks, the Mexicans, and the poor in general were discriminated against ferociously in the States, and that political opposition of any kind to the Establishment was becoming increasingly dangerous. But what counted as far as he was concerned was that it was not the same *sort* of class system.

Born of a working-class family in the indescribably ugly city of Doncaster, Martels had been cursed from the outset with a working-class Midlands dialect which excluded him from the "right" British circles as permanently and irrevocably as if he had been a smuggled Pakistani immigrant. No "public" school had been financially available to his parents to help him correct the horrible sound of his own voice; nor to give him the classical languages which in his youth had still been necessary for entry into Oxford or Cambridge.

Instead, he had ground, kicked, bitten, and otherwise fought his way through one of the new redbrick polytechnics. Though he emerged at the end with the highest possible First in astrophysics, it was with an accent still so atrocious as to deny him admittance to any but the public side—never the lounge or saloon—of any bar in Britain.

In the States, on the other hand, accents were regarded as purely regional, and a man's education was judged not by his inflection but by his grammar, vocabulary, and the state of his knowledge. To be sure, Martels was disturbed by the condition of the Negro, the Mexican, and the poor, but since he was none of these things, he was not oppressed by it.

As for political activity, that was absolutely out for Martels; he was an alien here. Were he to so much as raise a placard, regardless of what was written on it, he would lose either his passport or his citizenship.

The money situation had worked out in very much the same way. While there was a lot more of it available here than there was in England, in places like New York they took it away from you almost faster than you could make it; but Martels was not in New York. After a brief but moderately spectacular lecture-ship as a radio astronomer at Jodrell Banks, he had been hired on as Director of Research in the field by a new but already sprawling university in the American midwest, where money went a good deal farther—and where, in addition, Negroes, Mexicans, and the poor were in invisibly short supply. He could not quite put their plight out of his mind, but at least it was easier on the conscience to have it out of sight. The sailplaning here wasn't as good as it had been in the Chiltern Hills, but you can't have everything.

And there had been a final inducement: Sockette State had just completed construction of a radio telescope of a radically new design, a combination of mile-square dipole arrays and steerable dish with a peculiar, bowl-like glacial gouge in the landscape which made all its predecessors seem as primitive as the optical machine Galileo had filched from Hans Lippershey. The combination made it possible to mount a dish rather smaller than the one at Jodrell Banks, and involved instead a wave-guide focal point almost as big, and as skeletal, as the tubular frame of a 65-inch optical reflecting telescope. It took a startling amount of power to drive the thing—over and above the power necessary to steer it—but in theory at least, it ought to penetrate far enough around the universe to pick up the radio equivalent of the temperature at the back of Martels' own neck.

At first sight, he had been as pleased with it as a father who has just bought his son a new electric train. Just trying to imagine what great events might be recorded by such an instrument was splendid. It seemed to pose only one problem: Thus far, it couldn't be made to pick up anything but the local rock-and-roll station.

There was nothing wrong with the theory, of that he was quite certain. The design was as sound as it could possibly be. So was the circuitry; he had tested that out repeatedly and intensively. The only other possibility was a flaw in the gross construction of the telescope, probably something so simple as a girder out of true in the wave guide which would distort either the field or the transmission.

Well, there was at least one thing to be said for a redbrick university: It did nothing for either your Greek or your English, but it insisted that its physical scientists also be passable engineers before it let you graduate. Warming up the amplifier, tuning it, and cranking the gain up all the way—a setting which should have effectively relocated the campus of Sockette State in the heart of Ursa Major No. 2, a cluster of galaxies half a billion light-years away—he crossed the parabolic aluminum basketwork of the steerable antenna and scrambled up the wave guide, field strength detector in hand; awkwardly, it was too big to be put into a pocket.

Gaining the lip of the wave guide, he sat down for a rest, feet dangling, peering down the inside of the tube. The program now was to climb down into there slowly in a tight spiral, calling out the field intensity readings at intervals to the technicians on the floor.

Redbrick polytechnics insist that their physical scientists also be engineers, but they neglect to turn them into steeplejacks as well. Martels was not even wearing a hard hat. Settling one sneakered foot into what appeared to be a perfectly secure angle between one girder and another, he slipped and fell headlong down the inside of the tube.

He did not even have time to scream, let alone hear the shouts of alarm from the technicians, for he lost consciousness long before he hit bottom.

In fact, he never hit bottom at all.

It would be possible to explain exactly and comprehensively what happened to John Martels instead, but to do so would require several pages of expressions in the metalanguage invented by Dr. Thor Wald, a Swedish theoretical physicist who unfortunately was not scheduled to be born until the year 2060. Suffice it to say that, thanks to the shoddy workmanship of an unknown welder, Sockette State's radical new radio telescope did indeed have an unprecedented reach—but not in any direction that its designers had intended, or could even have conceived.

"Ennoble me with the honor of your attention, immortal Qvant."

Swimming upward from blackness, Martels tried to open his eyes, and found that he could not. Nevertheless, in a moment he realized that he could see. What he saw was so totally strange to him that he tried to close his eyes again, and found he could not do that, either. He seemed, in fact, completely paralyzed; he could not even change his field of view.

He wondered briefly if the fall had broken his neck. But that shouldn't affect his control of his eye muscles, should it? Or of his eyelids?

Besides, he was not in a hospital; of that much, at least, he could be sure. What was visible to him was a vast, dim hall in bad repair. There seemed to be sunlight coming from overhead, but whatever there was up there that was admitting it was not letting much through.

He had a feeling that the place ought to be musty, but he seemed to have no sense of smell left. The voice he had heard, plus a number of small, unidentifiable echoes, told him that he could still hear, at least. He tried to open his mouth, again without result.

There seemed to be nothing for it but to take in what little was visible and audible, and try to make as much sense as possible of whatever facts that brought him. What was he sitting or lying upon? Was it warm or cool? No, those senses were gone too. But at least he did not seem to be in any pain—though whether that meant that that sense was gone too, or that he was either drugged or repaired, couldn't be guessed. Nor was he hungry or thirsty—again an ambiguous finding.

About the floor of the hall within his cone of vision was a scatter of surpassingly strange artifacts. The fact that they were at various distances enabled him to establish that he could at least still change his depth of focus. Some of the objects seemed to be more decayed than the hall itself. In a number of instances the state, if any, of decay was impossible to judge, because the things seemed to be sculptures or some other kind of works of art, representing he knew not what, if anything at all, for representational art had been out of fashion all his life, anyhow. Others, however, were plainly machines; and though in no case could he even guess their intended functions, he knew corrosion when he saw it. This stuff had been out of use a long, long time.

Something was still functioning, though. He could hear the faintest of continuous hums, like a 50-cycle line noise. It seemed to come from somewhere behind him, intimately close, as though some spectral barber were applying to the back of his skull or neck a massaging device intended for the head of a gnat.

He did not think that the place, or at least the chamber of it that he seemed to be in, was exceptionally large. If the wall that was visible to him was a side rather than an end—which of course he had no way of determining—and the remembered echoes of the voice were not misleading, then it could not be much bigger than one of the central galleries in the Alte Pinakothek, say the Rubens room. . . .

The comparison clicked neatly into place. He was in a museum of some sort. And one both without maintenance and completely unpopular, too, for the floor was thick with dust, and there were only a few footprints in that, and in some cases none at all, near the exhibits (if that was what they were). The footprints, he registered without understanding, were all those of bare feet.

Then, there came that voice again, this time with rather a whining edge to it. It said:

"Immortal Qvant, advise me, I humbly pray."

And with a triple shock, he heard himself replying:

"You may obtrude yourself upon my attention, tribesman."

The shock was triple because, first of all, he had had no intention or sensation of either formulating the reply or of uttering it. Second, the voice in which it came out was most certainly not his own; it was deeper, and unnaturally loud, yet seemed to be almost without resonance. Third, the language was one he had never heard before in his life, yet he seemed to understand it perfectly.

Besides, my name is not and has never been Qvant. I don't even have a middle initial.

But he was given no time to speculate, for there now sidled into sight, in a sort of cringing crouch which Martels found somehow offensive, something vaguely definable as a human being. He was naked and dark brown, with what Martels judged to be a mixture of heredity and a deep tan. The nakedness also showed him to be scrupulously clean, his arms short, his legs long, his pelvis narrow. His hair was black and crinkled like a Negro's, but his features were Caucasoid, except for an Asian eyelid fold, rather reminding Martels of an African bushman—an impression strengthened by his small stature. His expression, unlike his posture, was respectful, almost reverent, but not at all frightened.

"What would you have of me now, tribesman?" Martels' new voice said.

"Immortal Qvant, I seek a ritual for the protection of our

maturity ceremonies from the Birds. They have penetrated the old one, for this year many of our new young men lost their eyes to them, and some even their lives. My ancestors tell me that such a ritual was known in Rebirth Three, and is better than ours, but they cannot give me the details."

"Yes, it exists," Martels' other voice said. "And it will serve you for perhaps two to five years. But in the end, the Birds will penetrate this too. In the end, you will be forced to abandon the ceremonies."

"To do this would also be to surrender the afterlife!"

"That is doubtless true, but would this necessarily be a great surrender? You need your young men here and now, to hunt, procreate, and fight the Birds. I am barred from any knowledge of the afterlife, but what gives you any assurance that it is pleasant? What satisfactions can remain for all those crowded souls?"

In some indefinable way, Martels could tell from Qvant's usage that "birds" was capitalized; he had caught no hint of this in the speech of the petitioner, whose expression had now changed to one of subdued horror. He noticed also that Qvant spoke to the presumable savage as anyone would address an educational equal, and that the naked man spoke in the same way. But of what use was the information? For that matter, what was Martels, presumably a man miraculously recovering from a major accident, doing in a moldering museum, help-lessly eavesdropping upon an insane conversation with a naked "tribesman" who asked *quaestiones* like a medieval student addressing St. Thomas Aquinas?

"I do not know, immortal Qvant," the petioner was saying. "But without the ceremonies, we shall have no new generations of ancestors, and memory in the afterlife fades rapidly. Who in the end should we have left to advise us but yourself?"

"Who indeed?"

From the faint tone of irony in his voice, Qvant had probably intended the question to be rhetorical, but in any case Martels had had enough. Mustering every dyne of will power he could manage to summon, he strove to say:

"Will somebody kindly tell me what the hell is going on here?"

It came out, and in his own voice, though without any physical sensation of speaking. And in that same unknown language, too.

There was a moment of complete silence after the echoes died, during which Martels felt a sensation of shock which he was sure was not his own. Then the petitioner gasped and ran.

This time, Martels' eyes tracked, though not of his own volition, following the fleeing man until he had vanished through a low, groined, sunlit doorway beyond which was what appeared to be a dense green forest or jungle. His guess at the size and shape of the hall was thus confirmed, and he now knew also that it was at ground level. Then his eyes returned to their stony and boring regard of the facing wall and the neglected, meaningless artifacts.

"Who are you?" the Qvant voice said. "And how have you invaded my brain?"

"*Your* brain?"

"This is my brain, and I am its rightful occupant—the precious personality of a master spirit, embalmed and treasured up on purpose to a life beyond life. I have been thus encased and maintained since the end of Rebirth Three, of which era what you see is the museum. The men of Rebirth Four regard me as a quasi god, and they do well to do so." The menace in that last sentence was unmistakable. "I repeat, who are you, and how have you come here?"

"My name is John Martels, and I haven't the faintest idea how I got here. And nothing I've seen or heard makes the faintest sense to me. I was within a couple of seconds of

2

certain death, and then suddenly, here I was. That's all I know."

"I caution you to tell the truth," Qvant said heavily. "Else I shall dispossess you, and then you will die within two or three seconds—or go on to the afterlife, which amounts to the same thing."

Martels felt an instant flash of caution. Despite the fact that the two of them seemed to share the same brain, this creature evidently could not read Martels' mind, and there might well be some advantage to be gained in withholding some of what little information he had. He had, after all, no guarantee that Qvant would not "dispossess" him anyhow, once the "quasi god's" curiosity was satisfied. Martels said, with a desperation more than half-real:

"I don't know what it is you want to know."

"How long have you been lurking here?"

"I don't know."

"What is your earliest memory?"

"Of staring at that wall."

"For how long?" Qvant said implacably.

"I don't know. I didn't think to count the days. Nothing ever seemed to happen, until your petitioner spoke."

"And what did you hear of my thoughts during that time?"

"Nothing I could understand," Martels said, being extremely careful not to hesitate after "nothing." Strange as it was to find himself apparently talking to himself like a split personality, it was stranger still to realize that neither psyche could read the mind of the other—and, somehow, immensely important that Qvant's opposite assumption should not be brought into question.

"That is not surprising. Yet I sense an anomaly in yours. You have the mind of a young man, but there is an aura about it which paradoxically suggests that it is even older than mine. To which Rebirth do you belong?"

"I'm sorry, but the question is completely meaningless to me."

"In what year were you born, then?" Qvant said, with obvious surprise.

"Nineteen-fifty-five."

"By what style of dating?"

"Style? I don't understand that either. We called it A.D., *Anno Domini,* after the birth of Christ. Insofar as anybody could be sure, He was born about seventeen thousand years after the human race invented written records."

There was quite a long silence after this. Martels wondered what Qvant was thinking. For that matter, he wondered what he himself was thinking; whatever it was, it was nothing useful. He was an alien personality in someone else's brain, and that someone else was talking nonsense to him—someone whose prisoner he was, and who also seemed to be a prisoner, though at the same time he claimed to be a sort of god, and Martels had seen him being consulted as one. . . .

"I see," Qvant said suddenly. "Without the central computer I cannot be accurate, but precision seems hardly necessary here. By your system, the present year is roughly 25,000 A.D."

This last shock Martels could not take. His insecurely re-embodied mind, still aquiver with the sick edginess of its escape from death, bombarded with meaningless facts, now under a new threat of death whose very nature he could not begin to comprehend, went reeling back toward the pit.

And at the same instant, it was assaulted, with cold, wordless ferocity. Qvant *was* going to throw him out.

Never before had he even dreamed it possible that a man could be thrown out of his own mind by someone else—and this was not even his own mind; here, he was the interloper. There seemed to be no way to resist, nothing that he could even grab hold of—even had he been inhabiting his own brain, he would have known no better than any other man of his time in what part of it his psyche resided. Qvant knew, that was evident, and was homing upon it with the mercilessness of a guided missile; and the terrible, ousting pressure was entirely emotional, without the faintest semantic cue which might have helped Martels to fight back.

The rotting hall wavered and vanished. Once more, Martels was without sight, without hearing. By instinct alone, he dug into . . . something . . . and held hard, like a crab louse resisting being shaken off the hide of a jackal.

The terrible battering went on and on. There was in the end nothing to cling to at all but a thought, one single thought: *I am I. I am I. I am I.*

And then, slowly, miraculously, the attack began to subside. As before, sound returned first, the faint ambiguous echoes of the museum; and then, sight, the sight of that same stretch of wall and floor, and those same lumpy monuments to and mementos of some far past in Martels' even farther future.

"It appears that I cannot be rid of you yet," Qvant said. The tone of his amplified voice seemed to hover somewhere between icy fury and equally icy amusement. "Very well; we shall hold converse, you and I. It will be a change from being an oracle to tribesmen. But sooner or later, Martels-from-the-past, sooner or later I shall catch you out—and then you will come to know the greatest thing that I do not know: what the afterlife is like. Sooner or later, Martels . . . sooner or later . . ."

Just in time, Martels realized that the repetitions were the hypnotic prelude to a new attack. Digging into whatever it had been that he had saved himself with before, that unknown substrate of the part of this joint mind that belonged to him alone, he said with equal iciness:

"Perhaps. You have a lot to teach me, if you will, and I'll listen. And maybe I can teach you something, too. But I think I can also make you extremely uncomfortable, Qvant; you've just shown me two different ways to go about that. So perhaps you had better mind your manners and bear in mind that however the tribesmen see you, you're a long way from being a god to me."

For answer, Qvant simply prevented Martels from saying another word. Slowly, the sun set, and the shapes in the hall squatted down into a darkness against which Martels was not even allowed to close his unowned eyes.

3

Martels was alive, still, which was something to be grateful for; but it was hardly a famous victory. Qvant could not throw him out—as yet—but Martels still had no control over his eyes, or their eyes, except the minimum one of changing depth of focus; and it seemed either that Qvant himself could not close the eyes, or never bothered to. Always, except when the rare petitioner came into the museum, they stared at that same damn wall and the blobby things in front of it.

Furthermore, Qvant never slept, and therefore, neither did Martels. Whatever mechanism kept the brain going in its un-viewable case, it seemed to make sleep unnecessary, which was perhaps fortunate, since Martels had no confidence in his ability to resist another of Qvant's attacks were he unconscious at the time.

This was just one of many aspects of their joint existence which Martels did not understand. Obviously, some sort of perfusion pump—that persistent tiny hum at the back of his head, like a sort of tintinnus—could continuously supply oxygen and blood sugar, carry away lactic acid, abolish fatigue. But it was Martels' cloudy memory that there was more to sleep than that: Dreams, for instance, were essential to clear the computer-analog that was the brain of the previous day's programs. Perhaps mere evolution had bred that need out of the race, although twenty-five thousand years seemed like a prohibitively short time for so major a change.

Whatever the answer, it could not prevent boredom, to which Qvant seemed to be entirely immune. Evidently he had vast inner resources, accumulated over centuries, with which to amuse himself through the endless days and nights; but to these, Martels had no access whatsoever. Martels concealed this fact as best he could, for it seemed increasingly important to him that Qvant's impression that Martels could overhear some of his thoughts should be encouraged; for all his obvious power and accumulated knowledge, Qvant did not seem to suspect the totality of the mind-brain barrier between them.

Nor would Qvant allow Martels to talk except when the two of them were alone, and mostly not even then. He seemed essentially incurious, or preoccupied, or both; and months went by between petitioners. Between the rare apparitions of the brown savages, the few new things Martels was able to learn were mostly negative and useless.

He was helpless, and that was most thoroughly that. Every so often, he found himself almost wishing that this mad nightmare should end with the shattering impact of his own unprotected head upon the center of the radio-telescope dish, like that merciless story that Ambrose Bierce had written about an incident at Owl Creek Bridge.

But occasionally there were the petitioners, and during their visits Martel listened and learned, a little. Even more rarely, Qvant had sudden, abortive bursts of loquaciousness, which were rather more productive of information, though always frustrating in the end. During one of these, Martels found himself allowed to ask:

"What was that business with the first tribesman that I saw —the one who wanted a protective ritual? Were you really about to give him some kind of rigmarole?"

"I was, and it would not have been a rigmarole," Qvant said.

"It would have been an entirely functional complex of diagrams and dances. He will come back for it in due course."

"But how could it possibly work?"

"Between any two events in the universe which are topologically identical there is a natural affinity or repulsion, which can be expressed in diagrammatic form. The relationship is dynamic, and therefore must be acted out; whether attraction or repulsion occurs depends entirely upon the actions. That is the function of the dances."

"But that's magic—sheer superstition!"

"On the contrary," Qvant said. "It is natural law, and was practiced successfully for many centuries before the principles behind it were formulated. The tribesmen understand this very well, although they would not describe it in the same terms I have. It is simply a working part of their lives. Do you think they would continue to consult me if they found that the advice that I gave them did not work? They are uncivilized, but they are not insane."

And, upon another such occasion:

"You seem to accept the tribesmen's belief that there is really a life after death. Why?"

"I accept it on the evidence; the tribesmen communicate regularly and reliably with their recent ancestors. I have no personal experience in this field whatsoever, but there is also a sound theoretical basis for it."

"And what's that?" Martels said.

"The same principle which allows both of us to inhabit the same brain. The personality is a semistable electromagnetic field; to remain integrated, it requires the supplementary computing apparatus of a brain, as well as an energy source such as a body, or this case we live in, to keep it in its characteristic state of negative entropy. Once the field is set free by death, it loses all ability to compute and becomes subject to normal entropy losses. Hence, slowly but inevitably, it fades."

"Still, why have you had no personal experience of it? I should have thought that originally—"

"The discovery," Qvant said, in a voice suddenly remote, "is relatively recent. No such communication is possible except along the direct ancestral line, and my donors—whoever they were—had dissipated centuries before the mere possibility was known."

"Just exactly how old are you, anyhow?" Martels said. But Qvant would say no more.

That conversation, however, did give Martels a little further insight into the characters of the tribesmen, and together with some other bits and scraps of evidence, a vague picture of history as well. Various references to "Rebirths" had enabled him to guess that civilization had been destroyed and rebuilt four times since his own period, but had emerged each time much changed, and each time less viable. Rebirth II had apparently been snuffed out by a worldwide glaciation; inevitably, Rebirth III had taken the form of a tightly organized, high-energy culture upon a small population base.

Now, however, the whole Earth, except for the Poles, was at the height of a tropical phase. Some of the technological knowledge of Rebirth III was still here in the museum in which Martels was doubly imprisoned, a fraction of it still intact and a rather larger fraction not too far decayed to be unrecoverable by close study. But the tribesmen of Rebirth IV had no use for it. Not only did they no longer understand it, but they thought it not worth understanding or salvaging. The fact that food was to be had for the picking or hunting with relative ease made machinery unnecessary to them—and their legends of what Rebirth III had been like made machinery repugnant to them as well. Their placid, deep-jungle kind of economy suited them very well.

But there was more to it than that. Their outlook had undergone a radical change which could only be attributed to the discovery of the real existence of the ghosts of their ancestors. It had become mystical, ritualistic, and in a deep sense ascetic —that is, they were death-oriented, or afterlife-oriented. This explained, too, the ambiguity of their attitude toward Qvant. They respected, indeed were awed by, the depth of his knowledge, and called upon it occasionally for solutions to problems which were beyond their understanding—so far beyond as to override their fierce sense of individuality; yet worshiping him was out of the question. Toward an entity which had no rapport with its ancestors, had never even once experienced such a rapport, and seemed destined never to have an afterlife of its own, they could feel only pity.

Doubtless it occasionally occurred to a few of them that even the apparently indestructible brain-case could not be immune to something really major in the way of disasters, such as the birth of a volcano immediately under the museum itself; but Qvant had been there, insofar as their own legends could attest, forever already; and their own lives were short. The death of Qvant was not in the short-term future of which they were accustomed to think.

Most of Qvant's conversation, however, was far less revealing. He seemed to be almost permanently in a kind of Zen state, conscious of mastery and at the same time contemptuous of it. Many of his answers to petitioners consisted only of abrupt single sentences which seemed to have no connection whatsoever with the question that had been asked. Occasionally, too, he would respond with a sort of parable which was not one whit more comprehensible for being longer. For example:

"Immortal Qvant, some of our ancestors now tell us that we should clear some of the jungle and begin to sow. Others tell us to remain content with reaping. How should we resolve this conflict?"

"When Qvant was a man, twelve students gathered upon

a cliff-side to hear him speak. He asked of them what they would have him say that they could not hear from their own mouths. All replied at once, so that no single reply could be heard. Qvant said: 'You have too many heads for one body,' and pushed eleven of them over the cliff."

Humiliatingly for Martels, in such situations the tribesmen always seemed to understand at once whatever it was Qvant was conveying, and to go away satisfied with it. On that particular occasion, though, Martels had managed to come up with an inspired guess:

"Obviously, agriculture can't be revived under these conditions."

"No," Qvant said. "But to what particular conditions do you refer?"

"None, I don't know anything about them. In fact, agriculture amidst jungle ecologies was quite common in my time. I could just somehow sense that that was what you meant."

Qvant said nothing further, but Martels could indeed feel, although dimly, his disturbance. Another phantom brick had been laid upon the edifice of Qvant's belief that he had less than total privacy from Martels.

Of course Qvant had deduced almost immediately from the nature and phraseology of most of Martels' questions that Martels had been some infinitely primitive equivalent of a scientist, and furthermore that Martels' eavesdropping did not go deep enough to penetrate to Qvant's own store of scientific knowledge. Sometimes, Qvant seemed to take a perverse pleasure in answering Martels' questions in this area with apparent candor and at the same time in the most useless possible terms:

"Qvant, you keep saying you will never die. Barring accidents, of course. But surely the energy source for this brain-case apparatus must have a half-life, no matter how long it is, and the output will fall below the minimum necessary level *some* day."

"The source is not radioactive and has no half-life. It comes from the Void, the origin—in terms of spherical trigonometry —of inner space."

"I don't understand the terms. Or do you mean that it taps continuous creation? Has that been proven to go on?"

This term was in turn unfamiliar to Qvant and for once he was curious enough .to listen to Martels' explanation of the "steady state" theory of Fred Hoyle.

"No, that is nonsense," Qvant said at the end. "Creation is both unique and cyclical. The origin of inner space is else-where, and not explicable except in terms of general juganity —the psychology of the wavicle."

"*The* wavicle? There's only one?"

"Only one, though it has a thousand aspects."

"And it thinks?" Martels said in astonishment.

"No, it does not think. But it has will, and behaves accord-ingly. Understand its will, and you are the master of its behav-ior."

"But how does one tap this power, then?"

"By meditation, initially. Thereafter, it cannot be lost."

"No, I mean how does the machine—"

Silence.

Martels was learning, but nothing he learned seemed to get him anywhere. Then, one year, a petitioner asked another question about the Birds; and when in all innocence Martels asked afterward, "What are these Birds, anyhow?" the levin-stroke of hatred and despair which stabbed out of Qvant's mind into his own told him in an instant that he had at long last happened upon something absolutely crucial—

If only he could figure out how to use it.

4

So obvious was the depth of Qvant's emotions, into which were mixed still others to which Martels could put no name, that Martels expected no reply at all. But after a pause not much more than twice as long as usual, Qvant said:

"The Birds are humanity's doom—and mine and yours, too, eventually, my uninvited and unwelcome guest. Did you think evolution had stood still during more than twenty-three thousand years—even without considering the peak in worldwide circumambient radioactivity which preceded Rebirth One?"

"No, of course not, Qvant. The tribesmen are obviously a genetic mixture that was unknown in my time, and naturally I assumed that there have been mutations, as well."

"You see nothing but surfaces," Qvant said with steely contempt. "They show many marks of evolutionary advance and change which are beyond your observation. For a single, simple-minded example, at the beginning of Rebirth Four, when the jungle became nearly worldwide, man was still an animal who had to practice the principles of nutrition consciously, and the tribesmen of that time did not have the knowledge. As a result, no matter how much they ate—and there was never any shortage even then, not even of protein —they died in droves of a typical disease of jungle populations whose name would mean nothing to you, but which might be described as 'malignant malnutrition'."

"That was well-known in my time, and not only in jungle populations. We called it marasmus, but there were lots of local names: kwashiorkor, sukha—"

"None of these words, of course, has survived. In any event, shortly therafter there occurred a major mutation which made proper nutrition a hereditary instinct—as it has always been with wild animals, and presumably was when man was a wild animal. Probably it was domesticated out.

"Another change, equally radical and perhaps not dissimilar in origin, occurred after the formulation of general juganity toward the very end of Rebirth Three. It was then found that the human brain had considerable hypnotic and projective power usable without the intervention of any prehypnotic ritual whatsoever. The theory showed how this could be done reliably, but the power had been perhaps always latent, or it may have been the result of a mutation—nobody is sure, nor does the question seem to be of any interest now.

"In me, these powers are massive—because I was specially bred to heighten them, among many others—but their action among the tribesmen is quite the opposite, in that their rapport with their ancestors makes them peculiarly *susceptible* to such hypnosis rather than good practitioners of it. They have become patients rather than agents.

"The animals, too, have changed—and in particular, the Birds. Birds were always elaborate ritualists, and in the aura of pervasive ceremony and juganity characteristic of Rebirth Four, they have evolved dangerously. They are now sophonts—sentient, intelligent, self-conscious—and have an elaborate postprimitive culture. They properly regard man as their principal rival, and their chief aim is to exterminate him.

"In this they will succeed. Their chief drive is toward survival in the here and now; the tribesmen, on the other hand, are increasingly too interested in death itself as a goal to make effective antagonists for them, regardless of the fact that they are still man's intellectual inferiors by at least one order of magnitude."

"I find that hard to believe," Martels said. "We had humans in that stage in my time, operating that kind of culture—the Eskimos, the Australian aborigines, the South African bushmen. None of them were as aggressive as you imply the Birds are, but even had they been, they never would have had a chance against the pragmatic intellectuals of the period. In fact, when I left, they were on the verge of extinction."

"The modern tribesman is neither intellectual nor pragmatic," Qvant said scornfully. "He will not use machines, except for simple hunting weapons; his only major defenses are ritual and juganity, at which the Birds are instinctively expert, and becoming more so all the time. When they become also intellectually expert, the end will be at hand.

"And so will ours. I have detailed reasons, both theoretical and technical, to believe that once the human population falls below a certain level, the power which supports this brain-case of ours will begin to fail, and thereafter, the case itself will fall apart. Even if it does not, the Birds, if they win—as they are certain to—will have millennia to wait for it to fall apart by itself, which is not impossible. Then they will pick the brain to pieces, and goodby to both of us."

In Qvant's voice there seemed to be a certain gloomy but savage satisfaction in the thought. Martels said cautiously:

"But why? You represent no threat to them whatsoever that I can see. Even the tribesmen consult you very seldom, and never about effective weapons. Why should the Birds not ignore you altogether?"

"Because," Qvant said slowly, "they are symbolists . . . and they hate and dread me above all other entities in the universe as a prime symbol of past human power."

"How can that be?"

"How have you failed to guess that? I was the reigning Supreme Autarch at the end of Rebirth Three, bred to the task and charged with the preservation of everything that Rebirth Three had learned, whatever happened. Without access to the computer, I am incapable of discharging that entire duty . . . but it is nevertheless to that charge that I owe my present immortal imprisonment. And my doom—and yours—beneath the beaks of the Birds."

"Can't you prevent this? For instance, by hypnotizing the tribesmen into some sort of positive action against the Birds? Or is your control too limited?"

"I could exercise absolute control of a tribesman if I so desired," Qvant said. "I shall put the next one through some paces to dispel your doubts about this. But the tribesmen who come to consult me are far from being the major figures in the culturo of Rebirth Four, and even were they great heroes and leaders—which do not even exist in this culture —I could not change the cultural set, no matter what changes I made in the ways individual men think. The times are what they are; and the end is nigh."

"How long before the end?"

"Five years, perhaps; certainly no more."

Suddenly, Martels felt a fury of his own. "You make me ashamed to be a human being at all," he snarled. "Back in my time, people fought back! Now, here are your tribesmen, presumably intelligent and yet refusing to use the most obvious measures to protect themselves! And here are you, obviously the most intelligent and resourceful human mind in all of human history, able to take command of and help all the others, passively awaiting being picked to pieces by nothing but a flock of Birds!"

As Martels' passion mounted, he was abruptly possessed by an image from his early youth. He had found a fallen

robin chick in the scrawny back garden of the Doncaster
house, thrown out of the nest before it was quite able to
fly, and obviously injured—probably by one of the many starv-
ing cats of the neighborhood. Hoping to help it, he had
picked it up, but it had died in his hands—and when he
had put it down again, his hands were crawling with tiny
black mites, like thousands of moving specks of black pepper.
And it was to be *birds* that would supplant man? Bloody
never, by God!

"You have no knowledge whatever of what it is you are
talking about," Qvant said in his remotest voice. "Be silent
now."

Thanks to the deception, Martels knew the depths of his
own ignorance better even than Qvant did. But unlike Qvant,
passivity was not in his nature; he had been fighting against
circumstance all his life long, and was not about to stop now.
Qvant was immensely his superior, in every imaginable way,
but he would no more accede to Qvant's doom than he had
to any past one.

Not that he said so, even had Qvant let him speak any
further. What he wanted, chiefly, was not only to get the
hell out of Qvant's brain—which Qvant obviously also would
welcome—but back to his home century; and only in human
techniques were there any hints of possible help in this direction. That malfunctioning perisher of a radio telescope had
sent him up here, and that had been a human artifact; surely,
by now, there must be some simpler way of reversing the effect.

Qvant had proven himself incapable of ridding himself of
Martels simply as a nuisance in the present era, let alone
of sending Martels back; and even did he know of such a
way, it was bound to be more complicated than the simple
exercise of throwing Martels out into the sad, dimming do-

main of the afterlife—an exercise which Qvant had tried and
failed to manage.

No, more human help was urgently necessary, and it would
have to be sought from the tribesmen. They were, it was clear,
scientifically innocent, but they were certainly preferable to
the Birds, and besides, they had resources that Qvant did
not. Most of these resources—such as their contact with their
ancestors—were mysterious and problematical, but by the
same token, they were outside Qvant's vast field of knowledge,
and just *might* be applicable to the main problem.

And they were not savages. Martels had already realized
that much from the few petitioners that he had seen. If
these tribesmen were not the best samples of the men of
Rebirth IV, what might the best be like? It was essential to
find out, regardless of Qvant's opinion in the matter. Qvant
had never seen them in their own environment; all his knowledge of their customs, behavior, and capabilities had come
from testimony, which is notoriously unreliable at its best,
from a sampling which he himself thought unrepresentative,
and from deduction. Nor did Qvant belong to this Rebirth himself; he might well be inherently incapable of understanding it.

Moreover, from his perspective, which was based upon
the dim past, Martels thought he saw things in the petitioners
which Qvant *was* incapable of seeing. Their intellects were
still operative, upon a level which was beneath Qvant's notice;
but which could be highly significant for Martels. Even a
brown man who struck him initially as the veriest savage
at one instant sometimes showed in the next some almost
supernatural talent, or at the very least some fragment of
knowledge which seemed to represent command of some entire field of science Martels' contemporaries had not even
known existed. These things might be used. They *had* to be
used.

But how? Suppose Martels were wholly in charge of the

brain which went under the name of Qvant; how could he
ask enough questions of the petitioners to find out anything he needed to know without arousing instant suspicion?
After all, the petitioners were used to having the questions
flow the other way. And even if he managed to do that, to
in fact even masquerade successfully as Qvant himself, what
could he tell the tribesmen that might provoke some kind
of action against the Birds, let alone advising them how to
go about it?

At best, he would only provoke bafflement and withdrawal.
What he really needed to do was to get out of here and into
the world, in some sort of a body, but that was plainly out
of the question. His only option was to try to figure out
some way of changing an age, and then hope that the age
would find some way to rescue him.

Put that way, the whole project looked impossibly stupid.
But what other way was there to put it?

Necessarily, he went on as before, biding his time, listening,
asking questions of Qvant when permitted, and occasionally getting answers. Sometimes, he got a new fact which
made sense to him; mostly, not. And he began to feel, too,
that the sleeplessness and the deprivation of all his senses
but sight and hearing were more and more eroding his reason,
despite the dubious and precarious access of his personality
to the massive reasoning facilities of the Qvant brain. Even
those facilities were somehow limited in a way he could not
understand: Qvant had now several times mentioned having
been deprived of a connection with a computer which would
have enabled him to perform even better. Was the computer
in the museum, and Qvant's divorce from it simply a matter
of a snapped input line which Qvant was unable to repair?
Or did it lie far in the past, at the end of Rebirth III? Martels
asked; but Qvant would not answer.

And in the meantime, for most of the time, Martels had

to stare at the same spot on the far wall and listen to the same meaningless echoes.

The midsummer century wore on. A year went by. The petitioners became fewer and fewer. Even Qvant seemed to be suffering some kind of erosion, despite his interior resources: sinking, indeed, into some sort of somnambulistic reverie which was quite different from his previous state of constant interior speculation. Martels could no more overhear Qvant's thoughts than before, but their *tone* had changed; at the beginning, there had been an impression of leisurely, indeed almost sybaritic, but constant, meditation and speculation, but now all that came through was a sort of drone, like a dull and repetitive dream which could not be gotten beyond a certain point, and from which it was impossible to awaken.

Martels had had such dreams himself; he had come to recognize them as a signal that he was on the verge of waking up, probably later in the day than he had wanted to; they were the mental equivalent of an almost self-awakening snore. Qvant, instead, seemed to be sinking deeper and deeper into them, which deprived the always-awake Martels even of Qvant's enigmatic conversation.

It had been a dull life to begin with, up here in 25,000 A.D. The boredom which had now set in with it was reaching depths which Martels had never imagined possible, and it looked like there was worse to come. He did not realize how much worse it was going to be until the day came when a tribesman came to petition Qvant—and Qvant did not answer, or even seem to notice.

Martels failed to seize the opportunity. He was entirely out of the habit of thinking fast. But when, perhaps six months later, the next petitioner appeared—halfway through the five years Qvant had predicted would end with the triumph of the Birds—Martels was ready:

"Immortal Qvant, I pray the benison of your attention."

There was no answer from Qvant. The background drone of his repetitive daydream went on. Martels said softly:

"You may obtrude yourself upon my attention."

Qvant still failed to interfere. The tribesman sidled into view.

"Immortal Qvant, I am Amra, of the tribe of Owlshield. After many generations, the volcano to the west of our territory is again showing signs of stirring in its sleep. Will it awaken to full anger? And if it does, what shall we do?"

Whatever Qvant might know about the geology of the area from which Amra had come, it was as usual inaccessible to Martels. All the same, it seemed only the simplest common sense not to hang around any long-quiescent volcano that that was showing new signs of activity, whatever the specifics. He said:

"It will erupt in due course. I cannot predict how violent the first outbreak will be, but it would be well to change territories with all possible speed."

"Immortal Qvant perhaps has not heard recently of the situation of our poor tribe. We cannot migrate. Can you not give us some rite of propitiation?"

"It is impossible to propitiate a volcano," Martels said, though with rather less inner conviction than he would once have felt. "It is also true that I have received little news from your area for long·and long. Explain why you cannot move."

He thought that he was beginning to capture Qvant's style of speech pretty well, and indeed the tribesman showed no sign of suspicion as yet. Amra said patiently:

"To the north is the territory of the tribe of Zhar-Pitzha, through which I passed on my way to your temple. Naturally, we cannot obtrude ourselves upon that. To the south is the eternal ice, and the devils of Terminus. And to the east, of course, there are always and always the Birds."

This, suddenly, was the very opportunity Martels had been waiting for. "Then, tribesman Amra, you must make alliance with the tribe of Zhar-Pitzha, and with weapons which I shall give you, make war upon the Birds!"

Amra's face was a study in consternation, but gradually his expression hardened into unreadability. He said:

"It pleases immortal Qvant to mock us in our desperation. We shall not return."

Amra bowed stiffly, and vanished from the unvarying field of view. When the echoes of his going had died completely in the hall, Martels found that Qvant—how long had he been listening?—had taken over control of the voice box, with a distant, cold, and deadly laugh.

But all that the once-Supreme Autarch of Rebirth III actually said was:

"You see?"

Martels was grimly afraid that he did.

5

Nevertheless, Martels had picked up something else that was new; and now that Qvant was paying attention again—for however long that would last—Martels might as well try to pump him about it. He said:

"I thought it was worth trying. I was trained never to take any statement as a fact until I had tested it myself."

"And so was I. But that exacts no sympathy from me. These petitioners are my last contact with the human race —except for you, and you are worse than an anachronism, you are a living fossil—and I shall not allow you to frighten one of them away from me again."

"Compliments received, and I didn't think you would," Martels said. "I'm sorry myself that I scared him off. But I'm curious about some of the questions. From his references to the volcano and to 'the eternal ice,' I gather that his tribe is on the edge of Antarctica, in an area we used to call the Land of Fire."

"Quite correct."

"But what did he mean by 'the devils of Terminus'?"

"There is a small colony of men living in the south polar mountains," Qvant said, with something very like hatred in his voice. "They are, or should still be, survivors of Rebirth Three, who were supposed to maintain a small, closed high-energy economy to power, tend, and guard the computer which was designed to supplement my function. The tribesmen in the area call them devils because they rigidly bar entry from all the rest of the world, as they were instructed to do. But as I have told you, I no longer have access to that computer; and whether it is because the men of Terminus have degenerated and allowed it to break down, or whether they have deliberately cut me off from it, I have no way of telling."

So the jungle culture and the crumbling museum were not the end of the story after all! "Why don't you find out?" Martels demanded.

"How would you propose that I do that?"

"By taking control of the next petitioner, and marching him down there to take a look."

"One, because the route would take me through the country of the Birds. Two, because I cannot allow the brain to fall silent over the long period such a journey would take; by the time I returned—if I did—the petitioners would have abandoned me permanently."

"Rubbish," Martels said, giving the word a calculatedly sneering edge. "The loss of contact with that computer cripples you considerably, as you've told me over and over again. Getting back into contact with it had to be your first order of business, if it was at all possible. And if you could have done it, you would have. The present impasse suggests instead that you haven't got the hypnotic or projective powers to change the course of crawl of an insect, let alone a human being!"

Astonishingly, Qvant did not seem to lose his temper, rather to Martels' disappointment.

"In fact I do not," he said, even more astonishingly, "if by 'me' you mean the rather fragile jugamagnetic field which is my personality, ego, psyche, call it what you will. If that were not the case, instances of newly dead souls instantly seizing possession of another living body would be commonplace. Instead, there are only scattered, unconfirmable rumors of a few such possessions. These powers are a function of the brain, of the organ itself—and pre-eminently, of this brain. A physical substrate and an energy source are both required to use them.

"As I promised, I shall demonstrate them at the next opportunity, not because allaying your doubts interests me in the slightest, but only to abate the nuisance of your clumsy attempts at experiment. *How* to use them I certainly shall not show you. Now, silence."

Silence perforce descended; but Qvant had already been loquacious enough, and that had not been the first occasion when Martels had been grateful for it. Perhaps Qvant, too, did occasionally feel the pressure of loneliness or boredom, after all. Or perhaps it was just that, not being limited by the necessity to breathe, nothing prevented him from spinning out a sentence as long as he wished, and these immense periods went on to becoming speeches, without Qvant's really being aware of it.

And now Martels had a new program—to get through to Terminus, somehow. Surely even a remnant of Rebirth III, with energy and technology at its disposal, offered more help for his peculiar problem than could all the tribesmen of Rebirth IV.

Qvant's last remark had to be interpreted as meaning that Qvant already suspected Martels of having formulated exactly such a program, just to be on the safe side. No doubt Qvant would have refused to teach Martels how to use the hypnotic and projective powers anyhow, simply to prevent him from undertaking any further agitation among the tribesmen toward a campaign against the Birds; but Martels had also just finished announcing· in the plainest possible terms that had he been Qvant, he would have tried to reach Terminus, an announcement an intellect far feebler than Qvant's could not fail to have registered as something to guard against. And as a one-time Autarch, he would know a great deal better than Martels that it never paid to underestimate one's opponent. Even back in Martels' own time, it was a funda- mental assumption of games theory that the enemy's most probable next move was also likely to be the best one.

Against this Martels had no recourse but his ability to mask his own thoughts from his brain-mate, and lay his plans as best he could; to reshuffle his cards, rethink his position, plot alternate courses and hope for still more new data. Seen in this light, for example, the positioning of the museum exhibits within his cone of vision took on new meaning: Suddenly it had become important to assess their sizes and shapes, whether they were still mounted or had fallen over, whether they were intact or disjunct, and their exact distances from each other. The ones outside the cone didn't matter, except for the larger ones between the brain-case and the entrance to the hall, and these he mapped as precisely as possible from memory.

Beyond that, as always, he could only wait for the next petitioner, but this time he did not care how long that was delayed. The longer the interval, the more time he would have to consider every way in which his scheme might go wrong, how to deal with each possible failure-point, what other options he had if it failed completely all up and down the line, and finally, what his next moves were to be and his future might be like were it to succeed completely by first intention. Strategy and tactics had never been among his interests, but if there lay within him any latent talent for generalship at all, now was the time to develop it, with all deliberate speed.

As it happened, the next petitioner turned up only six months later—insofar as he could tell, for keeping a mental calendar of the invariable days was impossible, and in the seasonlessness of this midsummer century he was sure that he lost months as well. That, too, was just as well, for Martels had already reached the point where he had run out of alternatives and refinements, and was beginning to suspect that his major plot was starting to change from a plan of action into a wish-fulfillment daydream.

Qvant was instantly alert, not at all to Martels' surprise. There was the usual ritual salutation and response. Then, after the visitor had come into sight and identified himself as Tlam of the tribe of Hawkburrow, the tribesman's eyes went glassy, he seemed to freeze solid, and not another word came from him. At the same time, Martels felt a curious lightness, a loss of pressure, almost a vacancy, as if Qvant were no longer present at all. Martels tried to speak, and found that he could.

"Qvant, are you doing that?"

"Yes," said the tribesman, in an eerie burlesque of Qvant's voice colored by his own. What was oddest about it, Martels found, was hearing Qvant speak without the usual blare of amplification. "Watch further."

The tribesman turned away and begun to walk aimlessly about among the monuments, occasionally making meaningless gestures before one or another of them. Martels found that he could also make his eyes track to follow. He said:

"Is he aware of what's going on?"

"No," the tribesman said, performing an absurdly solemn pirouette. "I could make him aware, but I prefer not to alarm him. I shall return him to the same position from which he started, and when the episode is over, for him no time will have passed."

"I gather, then, that this is projection rather than hypnosis."

"Quite correct. Draw no hasty conclusions, however. You are powerless in any case, but should you make even the slightest attempt to take advantage of your present position, I should be back with you in the brain upon the instant—and thereafter will devote a sizable fraction of my attention to making you more miserable than you have ever been in your life."

Martels rather doubted that Qvant could much improve on the miseries of a Doncaster childhood, but he was more interested in noting that the statement and the threat contradicted each other. However, he made no comment. The wanderings of the possessed tribesman had already produced more footprints in the dust than had incalculable decades of preceding visitors, and Martels was busily fitting them together with the tribesman's height and length of pace into the metrical frame of his map. It now seemed wholly unlikely that Qvant had any idea just how much new information he was providing by his somewhat vainglorious demonstration.

"Well," Martels said, "it doesn't look to differ from effects of hypnosis well-known in my time, except that there wasn't any preliminary routine. I would have thought that you were still in residence here, so to speak, and that the 'projection' consisted only of the use of some kind of line-of-sight microwave broadcast to override the poor fellow's own brain waves."

"Quite possible, of course, but primitive and damaging," the tribesman said. "In a moment I shall show you the difference."

Qvant brought the tribesman back to exactly his original position. Without an instant's preparation or transition, Martels found himself looking at the brain-case from the outside.

As he had long suspected, it was transparent, and the brain inside it was as big as that of a dolphin, but he had spent many months preparing himself not to waste so much as a second in studying whatever it turned out to look like.

Keeping his new body rigid and expressionless as if in shock, he changed the focus of his new eyes to seek out the tube, or tangle of tubes, which had to lead to the perfusion pump. It was there: One tube, and it looked heavily armored. Well, he had expected that, too.

Leaping one step back and three to the right, he swung up from the floor the clublike metal object he had long ago selected, and hurled it straight at the juncture of pipe and case.

The tribesman's jungle muscles, hunting aim, and speed of reflexes proved both true and far faster than anything Qvant could have anticipated. The heavy missile broke nothing, but a ghost of pain cried out in Martels' own mind at the impact.

Two leaps toward the entrance, another swooping grab at the floor, one leap back toward the case. As Martels swung the new and still heavier object high over his head, he felt Qvant's mind frantically trying to snatch his own back, but the new club—once probably a bus bar, rocker arm, limb of statuary, who knew what?—was already coming down with every dyne of force that Martels could demand from Tlam's arms and back. It hit the top edge of the brain-case with a noise like a pistol shot.

The case did not even scar, but all traces of Qvant's groping, powerful psyche blanked out. Tlam/Martels was already at a dead run toward the entrance—and Tlam proved to be able to run like a deer. Together they burst out into the glorious sunlight, and at once Martels relaxed all control. In obvious and predictable terror, Tlam plunged into the jungle, dodging and twisting along paths and trails Martels would never even have suspected were there, and even growing exhaustion did not stop him until night had almost fallen.

For Martels, the ride was as beautiful as the one train

trip he had ever made through the Brenner Pass. At long
last he could sense moisture again, smell greenness and mold
and rot and vague floral odors, feel heat on his skin and the
pounding of bare feet upon strewn earth and the propriocep-
tive flexing of muscles. He even enjoyed the lashing of
branches, vines, and thorns as they fled. ·

Now Tlam was examining the dense undergrowth all around
him with swift but intense care, searching for hazards only he
could know. Then he dropped to his hands and knees, crawled
under a thicket of something with blade-shaped leaves and
clusters of white berries, sobbed twice, curled into a ball, and
fell asleep.

It had worked. It had worked perfectly—flawlessly. Martels
was out.

But for how long? There was no way of knowing that. The
risks were still grave indeed, from the past as well as the future. Though he had deduced from what he thought had been
good evidence that the reach of Qvant's hypnotic and projective powers could not be long, he did not know exactly how
long they were, or, for that matter, how far away from the
museum he now was. He had stunned Qvant, that much was
inarguable, but he did not know for how long. Nor did he
know how wide a divorce between Qvant's personality and
his own would really become *regardless* of the distance between them. The dubious evidence for telepathy of his own
century had suggested that it suffered *no* diminution with
distance.

Suppose—improbable though it seemed—his crude attack
had actually done some damage to the brain-case, or to the
perfusion pump . . . enough damage so that the brain itself
would eventually die? What would happen to Martels if Qvant
died?·

Over and over, he did not know. He would still need to·
exercise absolute vigilance against even the faintest of probes

from Qvant. All he could be certain of at the moment was that at last he had a body. It could not exactly be described as his own, but at least it had given him back some freedom of motion.

Absolute vigilance . . . but what he had was a body, not a perfect perfusion pump, and he too was subject to its exhaustions. . . . Absolute vigilance. . . .

Martels fell asleep.

PART TWO

REBIRTH IV

6

Martels had strange dreams of falling down a tube lined with thornlike fangs, ending at long last in the vague, somehow dreadful expectation that when he opened his eyes, what he would see would be nothing but a dusty floor, lumps of statuary, and a not very distant wall. But as he struggled toward wakefulness, there crept into his nostrils the scents of damp earth and vegetation, and into his ears the rustling of a jungle, and he knew that that part of the nightmare, at least, was over.

He was at first surprised to find that his muscles did not ache after sleeping on the ground, but then he realized that they were not, after all, *his* muscles, and that Tlam must have slept in this fashion hundreds of times in his life. Since the tribesman did not seem to be awake yet, Martels delayed opening his eyes, but instead searched his own mind for the presence of Qvant. Falling asleep had been criminal carelessness; yet how could he have prevented it? In any event, he had apparently been lucky. Of the ex-Autarch he could find not a trace.

What next? Qvant had said that the way to Antarctica and Terminus was through the country of the Birds, but he could only have been talking about the most direct route—the one which would get him back to his own brain-case in the shortest possible time—for Amra, the petitioner who had appeared just

before Tlam, had come from a territory bordering on Antarctica and had reached the museum without having had to go
through Bird country. That suggested that Amra's territory
could not be unconscionably far away from the museum, for
surely the tribesmen would have no means nor any desire to
cross whole continents, let alone oceans, for the dubious bene-
fits of Qvant's cryptic advice. That they did not place a very
high value upon what Qvant told them had already been
evidenced by how seldom they asked for it, and what little
real good it seemed to do them in coping with the world they
had to live in.

Qvant had also confirmed Martels' guess that Amra's turf
lay somewhere near what used to be called Tierra del Fuego,
which in turn meant that the museum had to be situated somewhere in whatever was left of what used to be South America
—and that there was now a land bridge, or at least a stretch of
easily navigable water, between that once-island chain and the
ice-bound continent itself. All well and good; then the obvious
first step was passively to allow Tlam to go back to his own
tribe. Even if that lay at the worst due north of the museum,
Martels was so completely ignorant of tribal geography that
there seemed to be no other way for him to find out even so
much as which way due south lay. And, perhaps just as im-
portantly, which way was due east, which he already knew
from the testimony of Amra to be Bird country.

There might be much else to learn along the way, too—but
that raised another problem. Martels now had not only a body,
but a brain; but judging by his experience while semiliving
with Qvant, Martels would have no access to the specialized
knowledge within that brain without making himself known to
its owner, and then only with that owner's consent.

Thus far, apparently, Tlam did not know that he was ten-
anted at all; he had simply come to ask Qvant a question, had
instead committed a series of inexplicable acts of violence

against the demigod, and had fled as much in terror of himself as of the oracle. Martels, in revealing himself, might pose as an ancestor, or even as Qvant; and he already knew that he could resume control of Tlam's body whenever he needed to—

No, that wouldn't do. It would simply overwhelm Tlam, if it did not also panic him again, and there was probably just as much to be learned by continuing to go along for the ride. Best to give Tlam his head for as long as possible; the time when Martels would have to take it away from him would probably come all too soon, in any event.

Tlam stirred, and his eyes opened, admitting an extreme close-up of stems, creepers, toadstools, and things that looked like miniature cypress-knees. The tribesman seemed to come awake almost instantaneously. In lieu of stretching, he flexed his whole body, so sinuously that he did not shake a single leaf, and then peered out through the shrubbery. Apparently he saw nothing to alarm him, for he clambered to his feet without any further attempt at caution and proceeded to make a breakfast upon the clustered white berries. Their taste and texture most closely resembled boiled hominy grits which had been pickled for ten years in salted white wine through which sulfur dioxide had been bubbled, but it had been so long since Martels had tasted anything at all that to him they seemed delicious. Only a few meters away, Tlam found a huge blue chalice of a flower which was filled with dew or rainwater, warm and slightly sweet, but thirst-quenching nevertheless. Then, once more, Tlam began to run.

The tribesman kept moving steadily all the rest of the day. He paced himself like a cross-country horse: Run, trot, walk; run, trot, walk; run, trot, walk, with breaks of about ten minutes in every hour for a rest, a drink, a sticky fruit, or a pungent fungus. Though his route was necessarily very twisty, Martels was able to notice toward the afternoon that the filtered green-gold sunlight was fading to the right. A bonus! They were going south, at least roughly.

Not long before dusk, they came to an immense foaming torrent of a river which to Martels' eyes looked absolutely impassable, but it did not deter Tlam at all. He simply took to the trees, through which the river tunneled. Never before having seen a tropical rain forest or even read anything about one, Martels was astonished to discover that its treetops, entangled with thousands of vines, formed a separate and continuous world, as though the Earth had acquired a second surface, or some primitive vision of heaven had been lowered to within reach of the living. It was a heaven in which snakes masqueraded as vines, frogs lived and bred in the ponds formed by the corollas of immense flowers, monkeylike creatures almost as small as rats threw nuts with stinging accuracy and force, and green eyes in whose depths lurked madness sometimes peered out of darknesses which should have been in caves rather than in midair. But Tlam swarmed through it as though it were for him as natural a habitat as the jungle floor below, and by the time he touched ground again, the river was so far behind that it could not even be heard.

They spent that night on a sort of natural platform halfway up what proved in the morning to be a tree as contorted as an apple tree, but which bore fruits like walnuts. These Tlam casually crushed open in one hand two at a time, reminding Martels incongruously of an Italian dirty joke twenty-three thousand years old. After this breakfast, Tlam dropped to the ground and resumed their journey, but he was no longer running; he seemed to be in familiar territory and nearing his goal.

And then they were there. Before Martels' eyes lay what had to be a village, but like none he had ever seen before, even in pictures. Though the clearing which it occupied was quite large, a quincunx of ancient trees had been left standing in it, so that it was still covered by the densely matted roof of the rain forest. Placed regularly upon the open ground were heavy wooden shields, each of which was perhaps fifteen feet in diameter, face down and with their edges held up no more than six inches from the soil by thick wooden wedges which had been driven first through their rims and then solidly into the earth. The rims were circular, but the curvature of the shields, the mathematical part of Martels' mind noted automatically, was so nearly flat that were one to try to derive a value for pi over the convexity of one of them, it would probably come out to be exactly three point zero, just as the Babylonians had measured it.

Vines and lianas had been woven all over these very slightly bulging surfaces, and every strand bore thorns ranging from about the size of blackberry prickles to formidable spears nearly a foot long. Wherever possible, too, turf was exposed under the network, from which grew things like mutated nettles. The whole arrangement, from ground to jungle roof, was obviously a defense against attack from the air. Had Martels been in any doubt about that, it would have been dispelled at once by the Bird—each one some sort of hawk, from chick to monster—impaled upon the central spike of each shield, and by the stains at the tips of all the longer thorns, some of which were obviously dried blood, but the majority of different colors strongly suggesting painted poisons.

Considering what all this implied about the Birds, Martels was suddenly none too sure but that he would have been happier back in the brain-case. There, Qvant's comment that the Birds were dangerously intelligent had been only an abstraction. Here, there was living evidence that Tlam's tribe of Hawkburrow expected at any time a concerted attempt by Birds of all sizes—not just hawks—to be unshelled like a clam, or uncapped like a beer bottle.

There seemed to be nobody about, but Tlam paused at the edge of the clearing and gave a great shout. After what

seemed to be a very long while, there was a scrambling noise
and a semielliptical bite out of the edge of the nearest hut
lid lifted cautiously like the door to the tunnel of a trap-door
spider, and a face peered upward.

"Welcome alive, Tlam," the face said in a high voice, its
eyes squinted against the light, though its bald head was
still in shadow. The body that belonged to the head wriggled
out into the clearing and stood up. The villager turned out
to be a sturdy young woman, also naked, but also clean;
evidently the floors of the burrows were covered, not bare
earth.

Tlam said: "My thanks go with yours. I must see the Elders
at once."

The girl looked dubious. "They are sleeping after a night
hunt. Is the answer of the Qvant so grave that it cannot
wait?"

The Qvant. So it was a title. The discovery seemed to be of
no use—but there was no predicting when or if it might be.

"The matter is very grave, and will not keep. Rouse them.
That is my order."

"Very well." The girl dropped to her hands and knees and
slithered back into the hut again, not without a display that
reminded Martels that he once more had a body—and had
always had pretty bad luck with women. He forced his
thoughts back onto the main track. The girl's instant obedience
suggested that Tlam swung some weight here—might, perhaps,
even be some kind of chieftain. That could be helpful. Or
did the tribesmen keep slaves? That had never been mentioned, and it seemed extremely unlikely; the jungle would
have made escape too easy.

While Tlam waited, apparently at ease, Martels wondered
also about the night hunting. Slinking about with one's eyes
upon the ground, in the dark, unable to see any swooping
Birds, struck him as an extremely bad idea; and Tlam had

always carefully taken cover at dusk during their journey here. To be sure, almost all the birds of his own time that he knew anything about slept at night, but there had been nocturnal raptors, too; and one of Qvant's (the Qvant's) petitioners had mentioned owls. What a 250th century owl might be like was not a pleasant thought. But the fact that Tlam had not known that the Elders would be sleeping argued that night hunting was only an occasional and perhaps rare undertaking.

The girl appeared again, partway, and beckoned; then disappeared. Tlam crouched down promptly and crawled through the door.

The bowl under the shield proved to be surprisingly deep and roomy, and, as Martels had guessed, was carpeted, with what seemed to be stitched together hides, some with the fur still on them. They had been well tanned, for the only odor was the faintest of human pungencies, like that of slight and recent sweat. There was no light but the filtered daylight which leaked under the shield, but that was more than adequate rather dim, but even, and not at all gloomy.

Seven men were in the process of arranging themselves into a circle, and settling themselves into something very like the lotus position of Yoga. Despite their collective title, they did not look to be very much older than Tlam himself, as had probably been predictable among people whose life spans were short—though not, as far as Martels could judge, either nasty or brutish. Though they had only just been awakened, all seven looked completely alert, though several also looked annoyed.

Tlam went to the center of the circle and sat down himself. From this station, all the Elders were looking down upon him. Chief or not, he seemed to find this normal.

"What was the Qvant's answer, Chief Tlam?" one of them said, without preamble, "and why is it so urgent?"

"There was no answer, Elders, nor did I ever ask the question. The moment after I was allowed to obtrude myself upon the Qvant's attention, I found myself attacking him."

There was a murmur of astonishment.

"Attacking him?" the first speaker said. "Impossible! How?"

"With two objects from the museum floor, which I used as clubs."

"But—why?" another speaker said.

"I do not know. It simply happened, as though I were possessed."

"That is no excuse. No one is ever unwillingly possessed. Did the Qvant retaliate?"

"Not in any way," Tlam said. "Nor, of course, did I do him any harm. As soon as I realized what was happening, I ran—and he did not even attempt to prevent me."

"Of course you did the Qvant no harm," the second speaker said, with heavy emphasis. "But what harm you have done the tribe may be irrevocable. We do not know what would happen to us, were the Qvant to send his powers or spirit to seek us out! Even if he does not, we cannot petition him again while you live!"

"That is also my belief," Tlam said, with a serenity surprising until Martels remembered how death-oriented these people were. "And that is why I hurried to submit myself to your sentence."

Tlam bowed his head, and after that there was a silence which went on and on and on. Martels had unthinkingly anticipated some sort of discussion among the Elders, but instead not a word was spoken. Were they communing with their ancestors? That seemed to be the only likely answer. Martels would have liked to have looked around for the girl, but evidently she had remained by the entrance, and no help could be expected from her anyhow. It had been only an impulse—Martels was life-oriented.

At long last, the first of the Elders said, in a remote and sing-song voice:

"Chief Tlam, will you have blade or Bird, execution or exile?"

It was purely a ritual question, and in this culture could have only one answer. Instantly, Martels moved in on Tlam and suppressed it. He did not attempt to dictate another answer, but simply paralyzed Tlam's speech center entirely, as the Qvant had so often done Martels'. Distantly, he could sense Tlam's shock as the tribesman again felt himself possessed by something unknown and alien at a crucial moment.

There was another long silence, though not quite so long as the first. Finally, the first Elder said, in a voice dripping with contempt:

"How could we have been so mistaken as to have made *you* a chief? Our ancestors grow feeble, and our judgment as well. Your courage is less than a boy's. Let it be exile, then . . . and the memory, as the Birds tear you to pieces, that you were the first of all our tribe to fear the mercy of the blade. The punishment is far graver than the crime—but you yourself chose it."

In a moment of pity which he knew might be foolhardy, Martels promptly released Tlam to see if the deposed chieftain would enter any plea. But Tlam was obviously too shocked, humiliated, and completely confused to say anything, even had he wanted to. He crawled silently up the slope and out of the burrow. As he raised the thorn-edged flap, the girl spat on the back of his neck.

After that, he lacked the dignity even to hold the door up. The thorns raked him as it fell; he did not seem to care, or even to notice.

Standing, he looked about the clearing, blinking, tense, uncertain. It was plain that the situation was unprecedented—something that he had never even thought about in all his life. Under these customs, no other tribe would accept him;

he could not live long off the land by himself; he had inexplicably opted for exile—and had no place to go.

Should Martels take him over now? Martels would need the tribesman's instinctive knowledge and experience of how to live in the jungle; on the other hand, given his head, and given his attitudes, Tlam might well commit hara-kiri, or at best lapse into suicidal apathy. It was Hobson's choice.

Tlam himself decided against remaining any longer to await and face the contumely of the awakening village. He drifted despondently off into the bush. There arose in Martels' mind the verses of Goethe about the misanthrope which Brahms had set in the *Alto Rhapsody:* "The grasses rise behind him; the waste receives him." But it was not Tlam who had rejected men, but they him, and it was entirely Martels' fault.

And there was no help for it. At this point, to a vocal cry of horror and despair from Tlam, Martels set him to marching south, toward Terminus . . . and the country of the Birds.

At long last, the real journey had begun.

7

As they moved south, Tlam gradually seemed to become more fatalistic, so that Martels was warned by a sudden though slight increase in the tribesman's muscle tone when they actually crossed into what Tlam considered to be Bird country. But for several days thereafter, they saw no Birds at all; the pattern of marching, concealment, sleep, foraging, and marching again settled back into a routine which Martels allowed Tlam to dictate. No one observing the tribesman from outside could have guessed the dialectical tension between Tlam's dulling despair and Martels' increasing urgency which was the unspoken central fact of their inner life.

Then they saw a Bird. It was a little, dun-colored creature, disarmingly like a sparrow, but Tlam went into instant tetany at the sight, like a rabbit freezing at the sight of a snake. The Bird in turn bobbed up and down, its claws clinging to the outermost end of a low branch, cocking its head and flirting its feathers, and occasionally interrupting its regard to groom itself. Its gaze seemed to be virtually mindless, and after a while it gave an indifferent chirrup and shot up and away into the dimness of the rain forest like a feathered bullet.

It was hard to believe that such a thing could be dangerous, but cancer viruses also came in small packages. Tlam remained frozen for several minutes after it had vanished, and thereafter moved with still greater caution, constantly shooting glances from side to side and up and down with a quickness which was in itself almost birdlike. Nor was he wrong; for the next day they saw three more of the sparrowlike Birds, and the next day, five. And the morning after that, they emerged from their sleeping burrow to find a smoke-black thing like an enormous crow looking down upon them, just out of club's reach, its head bent, its neck extended until it seemed almost snakelike, its eyes glassy and unblinking.

Memories of *Macbeth* and Edgar Allan Poe would have made Martels shudder had he been in his right body, but Tlam was still nominally in charge, and he froze again. For very disparate reasons, neither of the two minds was surprised when the Bird's beak parted, its throat ruffled and pulsed, and it said in a voice like fingernails on a blackboard:

"Go home."

"I have no home any more," Tlam said hopelessly. "I am an outcast from my tribe, and all the tribes of men."

"Go home," the sooty thing said. "I lust for your eyes. The King has promised them to me if you do not go."

Curiously, this did not seem to frighten Tlam any further; perhaps it was a standard threat—or perhaps, if he had never been here before, he had already reached the limits of his terror. A line from James Thomson's *The City of Dreadful Night* came back to Martels: "No hope can have no fear." The tribesman said only:

"I cannot."

"The King hears."

"So be it."

"Go home."

"I cannot."

This exchange was threatening to turn into a ritual, and certainly was producing no more information. In growing impatience, Martels broke through Tlam's paralysis and set him to walking again, though not without allowing the tribesman substantial residues of his caution. The Bird did not move, let alone follow, but somehow Martels could feel its unblinking gaze drilling into the back of Tlam's neck.

After a while, however, Martels began to feel a surprising resistance to further travel—surprising not only because he had assumed that Tlam would have been as glad to get away from the Bird as he was, but for the unexpected strength of it. With some interest, he released control almost completely; if there was a reason for this much resistance, it was probably urgent for Martels to know what it was.

Tlam backed carefully into a bower where there was a huge tree at his back and a great deal of cover on all sides, plus a good deal of free space in front and above. His movements were more tentative than ever, as though he were suspicious of the degree of his new freedom, and expected to be taken over again at any moment. Martels let him settle himself to his own satisfaction without any interference whatsoever.

For a while, the tribesman simply rested; but at last he said in an almost voiceless whisper:

"Immortal Qvant, or spirit sent by Qvant, hear me."

Martels said nothing, though he had a deep, uneasy feeling that he ought to respond, if only to encourage the tribesman to continue. But apparently silence was no more than Tlam had expected. After repeating the invocation, he went on:

"I know not at all why you have had me driven from your presence, or caused me my exile from my tribe. Still less do I know why you have harried me like a sacrifice deep into the country of the Birds. I have done nothing to earn your hatred; my very madness in your temple can have been caused by none other than your immortal self, for surely my ancestors would never have countenanced it. Tell me what you want.

What have I done, that I should die for it? What is the doom that you have put upon me? How may I fulfill your wishes? Answer, immortal Qvant, answer, answer!"

The speech was not without dignity, but there was no answer that Martels could have given him, nor any hope for justice. In the light of Martels' own purposes, Tlam was even closer to being a sacrificial animal than he suspected himself to be. Neither of them had much future, but nothing that Martels could explain would make it seem brighter to Tlam. He could do nothing but remain silent.

"Immortal Qvant, answer me, answer me! What shall I do that you should be assuaged? Soon the Birds will hear my mind, and perhaps yours—or that of your creature. Then their King will have me, and he will question me to the death. What answers shall I give? What is the purpose of this possession? Must I die unknowing? I have not, I have not, not done anything to die for!"

That cry had been old when it had been torn from the throats of the *hoi polloi* at the sack of Syracuse. There was an answer—*You were born*—but there would be no point in offering it. It was too fatalistic to advance Martels' own quest one step, let alone to satisfy Tlam; better not even to confirm, at this juncture, Tlam's well-founded suspicion that he was possessed, by so much as one word.

Some patterns, however, never change. Tlam cried out, almost at full voice, for the ritual third time:

"Immortal Qvant, or spirit sent by Qvant, grant me your attention! Answer me, your petitioner!"

Martels continued to stand mute . . . but there was a slow stirring at the back of his brain, like the sensation of awakening slowly from a repetitious dream; and then his lips stirred, his chest rose, and his heart sank as he heard himself saying in an all too familiar voice:

"I am with you, tribesman . . . and your demon is not

of my sending. Press forward to its urging, nevertheless, and fear not the Birds. Our hour is yet to come."

The triple-minded man rose, and moved somnambulistically southward once more.

8

Martels did not need to have been an ornithologist to know that the formation flying, the migrations, and the homing instincts of birds had always been a mystery. His father, like many bottom-class Englishmen of his time, had raced pigeons, and had occasionally eked out his other income from the football pools, the darts, shove ha'penny, the betting shop (more politely known as "turf accountants"), and (when all else failed) the Labour Exchange by selling a favorite bird to another fancier. Back then, there had been a good many fanciful theories advanced to account for why homing birds behaved as they did, one of the most fanciful of which had been that the creatures had the equivalent of iron filings in their inner ears—or in their hollow bones—which enabled them to navigate directly along the Earth's magnetic lines of force.

That they were telepathic had naturally been one of the first of all of the hypotheses—and now, contrary to all of Martels' prior inclinations, he was prepared to believe that this was in fact the most tenable explanation. He did not like it any the better for its having been forced upon him.

Qvant did not speak again. The triple-minded creature that was Tlam forged steadily southward, without need of further urging from Martels, and under his own guidance, as before, as to how to handle the minutiae of the journey. Martels, withdrawn, continued to speculate.

Of course one would have to begin by throwing out all the 20th century observations on telepathy as resting solely upon testimony; every time a Rhine or a Soal took it into the laboratory, it evaporated into the clouds of these investigators' willingness to call unfavorable results by some other name. Direct contact with it, here, now, seemed to indicate that it was in fact subject to the inverse-square law, or, in other words, that it diminished with distance; and if birds—even the bird-brained birds of Martels' own time—had always been able to use it, then it had probably started as nothing more than a sort of riding light by which like minds and like intentions could be detected.

Such an ability would naturally be selected *out* in sentient creatures, since from the evolutionary point of view, intelligence would serve the same functions far better. That would leave behind only the maddening vestiges—a sort of vermiform appendix of the mind—which had so persistently disappointed the most sincere occultists from Newton onward. Maybe mob psychology was another such vestige; if so, that was definitely *anti*-survival and would be selected out even faster. Even for the Birds of this century, it did not have much future—but Martels was going to have to deal with them in the present.

Another question: How was Qvant tied to Tlam and Martels? Was he inside Tlam's skull, as Martels now seemed to be? Or was he still back in the museum inside the assaulted braincase, with only a tenuous spiritual tentacle stretched out to connect him to the tribesman, perhaps through Martels' own intermediation? By Martels' hypothesis, that ought to be impossible, but the men of Rebirth III might quite easily have bred telepathy back into the human line, as his own time had recreated the aurochs, and as Qvant's people had made Qvant

the bearer of hypnotic and projective powers. Qvant had
mentioned something called general juganity, "at which the
Birds are instinctively expert." What *were* the laws underlying
a phenomenon of this kind? Qvant doubtless knew them, but
they were impossible to deduce from scratch, at least by anyone who had been so complete a skeptic as Martels until he
had been plunged into this era, minus some twenty centuries
of intermediate thought on the subject.

Whatever those laws were, they seemed to confuse the
Birds. As the more and more neglected body of the triply-
inhabited man plunged on through the thorns, vines, and
fronds of the midsummer century, the Birds gathered about
it, pecking, darting, quarrelling, and slashing, yet never making the fatal final attack that Martels—and, clearly, Tlam—
expected at any moment. He felt like a steer being driven
down the slaughtering chute, unable to understand what
was going on, certain only that creatures whom he had regarded heretofore as not much more than minor nuisances
had suddenly and mysteriously turned malevolent.

Qvant did not help, nor even surface, but a faint and
complacent hum, like a maintenance turnover, somewhere near
Tlam's cerebellum or even farther down into the brain-stem
near the rhinencephalon warned Martels that he was still
there, in whatever mode. That was helpful, in a way, in that
he did not interfere with Martels' imposed *Drang nach Sueden;*
yet at the same time, Martels was sure that the furies of
tentative rage with which the Birds now surrounded them
like a storm of feathers had something to do with Qvants
immanence. After all, had not Qvant himself said that he was
a symbol of everything the Birds most hated and feared?
Martels was sure by now that a single man occupied only by
his own mind would have been shredded to bits out of hand
long before he had seen the first, ravenlike creature; the triple
being was being spared in part because the Birds sensed

something peculiar about it which they both hated and needed
to know—but could not tell by direct telepathy anything more
than that.

Thus it was that he came at long last to the Tower on
Human Legs.

He did not know the overall size of the museum in which
he had awakened into this world, but some sort of leakage
between Qvant's mind and his told him that the Tower was
considerably bigger. It had been erected in a natural clearing
so large as to be almost a meadow, and filled most of it with
its base, all of it with its shadow.

The three columns which held it aloft were, of course, its
most striking feature. Originally they had been very ancient
trees, each of which might have been made the core of a
respectable medieval tower in itself, with a spiral staircase
carved last of all out of the wood, like several such Martels
had seen in Paris. They formed instead the points of a nearly
equilateral triangle, with portions of their thick roots above
the ground. Perhaps it had been these roots which had originally suggested the conceit of shaping the pillars in the form
of human feet and legs, toes outward, around which the Tower
proper was draped like an exaggeratedly long tubular skirt.
Or perhaps the Birds had originally only girdled the trees
to stop their growth, and in flensing away the bark had ac-
cidentally uncovered a pre-existing resemblance, which was
heightened by the ivory whiteness of the wood underneath.
The work itself had evidently been done with something like a
drawknife, for Martels could see the flatness of the long strokes
it produced—a technique which had been cunningly used to
accentuate the flatness of the human shin.

The Tower proper had been fastened around the trees as a
series of drums of equal size, whose sides were crazy quilts
of animal hides beautifully stitched together with the finest
of leather cords. The hides themselves appeared at first to

have been chosen at random, but seen from a distance they flowed upward from the meadow in long twisting lines which gathered together toward the top of the structure like a stylized candle flame. Its point, however, was not visible from where Martels stood; more than likely, the total effect could be seen to best advantage from the air.

Even the main body was not easy to see amidst the clouds of Birds which constantly surrounded it, however; nor was Martels given any chance to study it in detail. He was chivvied under the immense tripod to its exact center, where there proved to be a slender central pole around which jutted a spiral of ascending pegs. Undignified, needlelike thrusts into Tlam's rump indicated that he was to climb these.

The pegs had not been cut or spaced for men, and since it got steadily gloomier as he climbed, for a while his attention was totally centered on keeping himself from falling. Eventually, he ran out of breath, and had to sit down upon tho next peg which looked to be thick enough to bear his weight, with assists from feet and hands on the two adjacent. Breathing heavily, he clung to the pole and pegs and looked aloft.

Above him there first seemed to be a barrel-shaped universe extending into infinity and pricked along its sides with the most intense of little stars, growing confusingly brighter with distance. Strange nebular masses occasionally occluded them, and there was a good deal of twinkling. Bars of light crisscrossed it, some of them being shed by the brighter stars, others looking more solid, and set at different angles, as though this universe had a visible metrical frame. The twittering, fluttering, and squawking of the Birds outside was here muted into a composite thrilling, an audible music of the spheres, which was shaken occasionally by some broader shudder or larger pinions.

After a while, his eyes became accustomed to the gloom and he began to see what was really to be seen. It was not

much less remarkable than his first impression, and the two
tended to change places abruptly, like an optical illusion.
The stars were meeting-places of the corners of hides; the
shafts were sometimes true sunbeams, as direct and intense
as laser light; and more seldom were the radial ribs of the
drums. These ribs, plus the increasingly larger pegs of the
ridgepole he was clinging to, provided an ascending series
of perches upon which sat great dusky raptorlike figures in
apparent somnolence except for an occasional shifting of claws
or flutter of wing or drooping tail. Here and there, eyes like
half-moons tilted and looked down upon him, filming and
closing, then opening again. There was a whole heirarchy
of Birds inside this tower—and Martels was in no doubt at
all as to who was at the top. This universe was theirs, every
mote and beam.

His honor-guard was gone now, and except for the half-
moons, nobody seemed to be paying close attention to him.
He looked down. The dun disc of the floor under the tower
looked like the far end of a tunnel in this artificial perspective
but the unique experience of having fallen down the barrel of
a telescope gave him reason to believe that it was a drop he
could survive, particularly if he began by swinging down
around the pegs again, monkeylike. And once he hit the earth,
he could probably scuttle flat along the meadow floor back
into the jungle faster than the Birds could realize that he
might. It seemed highly unlikely that any man had been drawn
this far into the Lobachevskian universe of the Birds, or at
least not for decades, and besides, they were probably not
equipped to appreciate how rapidly a man can revert to his
quadruped ancestors when driven by the need. Their own ancestors were bipedal dinosaurs even farther in the past.

But he would have to be quick. More and more half-moons
were regarding him now, and he felt an obsessive pressure
radiating out from the center of his mind, as though those

eyes were demanding his identity. Hitching forward until most of his weight was on his feet, he shifted and prepared for the long swinging drop through the black, feathery continuum. . . .

In midswing the vertical twinkling tunnel and the disc of dirt below it blacked out entirely, and for the second time Martels found himself in the midst of a mortal struggle with Qvant. The battle was wordless, which gave Qvant enough of an advantage to leave Martels no attention left over for his immediate environment. The riptides of demanding hatred surged through a featureless, locationless chaos in which the only real things were the combatants. They went at it over kalpas of eternity, eternities of seconds, neither knowing which was hammer and which was anvil, against no backdrop but a distant scream which might have been Tlam's.

They were still fighting when the tribesman's body hit the ground.

9

A deep, racking ache awoke Martels out of a sleep which he would infinitely have preferred to have been endless. He groaned and stretched tentatively. He had hit the bottom of the telescope, evidently; but why was it made of drumhide rather than fused quartz? But radio telescopes do not have quartz mirrors, either; why shouldn't there be drumhide instead? Whatever the reason, he could sense it flexing tautly as he moved, giving off a deep *ronronner*, like a cheetah purring in French. Far echoes answered it, as if from below.

There was light on his eyelids, but he did not open them yet, listening instead inside his own psyche for an unknown enemy. Qvant? The name brought everything back and he was instantly tense.

At the moment, there seemed to be no trace of the Autarch. A faint edge of alertness suggested that Tlam was also awake, and perhaps had been awake for some time. Well, that figured; the first *persona* to awaken from the shock of a long fall would be the tribesman, and Qvant, who had not been in a body for some centuries, would be the last. That was a point to remember: Against Qvant, physical pain was an ally.

Martels heaved himself up on one elbow and looked about. He seemed now to be in the topmost drum of the tower, one which was smaller than all the others and hence had been invisible from the ground. It had no central pole, only the radial ribs and circular members of the drum itself. Furthermore, it was open upon three sides, by panels which had simply been left off the drum entirely. The high chamber was uncomfortably cold, which made him realize that from having had no sensations at all in the brain-case he had gone to being uncomfortably hot all the time up to now. Didn't this damn century have anything but extremes?

He raised himself creakily to a sitting position and looked upward. By now he had realized that this direction, which nobody pays much attention to in normal life, was what counted in the country of the Birds. It could of course have been deduced, but getting into the habit was something else; like an Englishman who knows that Americans drive on the wrong side of the road, yet does not connect it with looking left instead of right when he steps off a curb.

Sure enough. At the topmost reaches of this cylindrical hat there was another perch, surrounded by cruel, thorny, occasionally shifting claws; then a long, greasy, feathery breast of blue-tinged black; and at last, sagging, narrow, reptilian shoulders and a long narrow beak topped by very narrow eyes. The thing looked like a gigantic vulture, but there were rings upon its eight scaly fingers; the nails of each central claw had been filed to a razor edge, and over its breastbone was embedded a gleaming metallic seal enameled with something very like the Taoist sign of Yang and Yin, the oldest symbol in history. The monster did not seem to be asleep; on the other hand, it did not seem to be watching him. It was just, terrifically and potently, *there*.

After Martels reached the nearest opening in the drum, Martels could see why. The drop from there to the setback was only about twenty feet, but the setback too had a drumhead floor which he would plunge right through; and from there, it was perhaps more than a thousand feet down through the cylindrical universe to the meadow.

The view from here over the forest would have been beautiful, had he been in any position to appreciate it, but it was contaminated by more Birds of all sizes at all possible distances, wheeling and wheeling. Clearly, as a captive he was something special.

Restlessly, he crossed to the next window. These openings seemed to be placed alternately to the legs on the ground. Essentially, the view had not changed here; he moved on to the last.

Still the same. No, not quite. The light was different. And more than that: There did not seem to be any horizon on this side; it was masked by what seemed to be almost a wall of mist, rising almost a third of the way to the zenith.

A stab of pure excitement shot through him, despite his best attempts to keep it from Tlam and from the problematical presence of Qvant. His astronomical training, his now lengthening experience with Tlam of jungle orientation, and even a vague memory of Poe's *Arthur Gordon Pym* combined like so many puzzle pieces.

He was looking due south over the Drake Passage toward the Palmer Peninsula of Antarctica . . . or what had been those other lands and seas in his time.

His mind reeling with unfocused desire, he clung to the edge of the ribs and sat down, suddenly aware in addition that his borrowed body was weak with hunger and accident, sticky and reeking with its passage through a thousand jungle saps and resins, aching with effort and parched with thirst. Above him, the enormous vulturelike creature brooded, semi-somnolent but obviously alert enough. There lay the Promised Land; but as far as Martels was concerned, the curtain of rising mist which marked the beginning of the icecap might as well be the layer of ice-crystals which delimited the atmosphere of Mars.

Had great gull-like Birds flown toward him out of the mist crying *Tekeli-li,* he could not have been more sure . . . or more helpless.

Behind the knowledge arose a faint current of mockery. Qvant was awake.

One of the wheeling Birds was approaching the tower; now that he noticed it, he realized that he had been subconsciously watching its approach for some minutes. Suddenly it was coming at him like a cannonball. He pulled away from the open panel, his back against the hides.

There was a thrashing of pinions above him as his guard moved to a higher perch. Another rush of feathers and disturbed air, and its place was taken by a scarlet and gold effigy nearly as tall as he was. It wore no insignia whatsoever, but none were needed; its plumage, its bearing, its very shape—a combination which suggested both the eagle and the owl, without closely resembling either—told him that this was the King.

The great Bird sat silently regarding him for several minutes, its eyes occasionally filming. At last the hooked beak parted, and a deep, harsh voice said:

"Who are you?"

Martels wondered if the King had any suspicion of how difficult that apparently routine question would be to answer. Under the circumstances, he felt that it would be best to let Tlam do the talking, provided that Qvant did not interfere. But Qvant showed no present disposition to intervene.

"I am nothing, Lord King. Once I was a man of the tribe of Hawkburrow, but I have been cast out as one demon-ridden."

"We see what you are," the King said. "It is the nature of your inner self we seek to understand. You are three in one, like this the footstool of our world. The tribesman is beneath our notice; he is but a son of Man. Who are these others?"

Martels had a flash of inspiration. He said in his own voice: "I, Lord King, am the tribesman's ancestor, far removed."

The King blinked, once. "We hear you, Father," he said surprisingly. "Yet we sense that though what you say is the truth, it is not the whole truth. We feel indistinctly in you the one human being in all our world who most threatens our coming triumph. For this alone we should kill you, and we shall—but what is this third spirit which we would so loose upon that world?"

Martels was almost as taken aback by the King's candidness as by the impossibility of understanding what he was saying. In that moment of indecision, Qvant's answer rushed smoothly forward with all the power of his ancient and continuous sentience, as implacable as a locomotive about to cut down a buttercup between the ties. Something monstrously evil about the formed yet unreadable thought evidently reached Tlam even faster than it did Martels. Together they clung about it, trying to close it in, like twin twinges of a weak and belated conscience.

Tlam's unexpected help seemed to be only about as effective as would have been the interposition of an additional buttercup before the onrushing engine. Qvant's voice said evenly, "I, Lord King, am the Qvant of Rebirth Three; and I spit upon your spittleless world and all its little lice."

This was certainly a speech Martels would have prevented Qvant from making, had he been able; yet Qvant's mind was full of sullen rage as he fell back, as if defeated, leaving Martels nearly sure that it had not been the evil thing the Autarch had had prepared to say.

The King bent his huge head and turned it slightly to one side.

"Why would the Qvant so seek to provoke us?" he grated.
"Here again is truth, yet not the whole truth. Were it wholly
so, we should by no means release that ageless spirit into
our future; but why does it go about in flesh, and further
cumbered with lesser selves? Why this trifold disunity? Whom
among you shall answer?"

Under any other circumstances, Martels might have opted
for the whole truth, in the hope of proving his harmlessness;
but the Bird King's own mind did not seem to be sufficiently
analytical to understand the answer, even—which was doubt-
ful—had he had enough historical background. Qvant, in
turn, was apparently still sulking; and as for Tlam, though
he was now to be regarded as a potential ally, he understood
least of all of them what was going on. Perforce, they all
stood mute.

"Very well," the King said. "We shall put the question to
the Talons."

With a buffeting flash of gold and scarlet, he was gone.
The vulturine guard resumed its perch.

The night came rapidly—evidently it was technically winter
in these high southern latitudes—and with it came the suspicion that the Birds were not going to provide any food or
water. A change of guard brought Martels no relief, unless
he counted a large, limey dropping left by the first sentinel,
evidently in contempt, since the floor of the drum was otherwise clean.

He scarcely worried; he had too much else to think about.
Some of the new knowledge seemed quite useless: For example, it was now confirmed that "Qvant" was a title, not a
name, but unless name-magic also counted for something in
this millennium, the confirmation left him no better off than
before. On the other hand, Martels' impression that the Bird
King's mention of "the Talons" implied physical torture had

been instantly and dramatically confirmed by a prolonged mental shudder from Qvant (no, *the* Qvant, never assume that any fact is useless until it is so proven)—which in turn at least suggested that Martels' original guess that pain might prove to be a useful weapon against the Autarch was probably right. Good; put that one in the active file.

The moon began to rise. Even low on the horizon, it was smaller than he had ever seen it before. Of course; tidal forces had been increasing its angular momentum for more than twenty-three thousand years since he had seen it last. He had not really been in any doubt of what century he was in now, but this confirmation gave him a small chill nonetheless. The pole star, it occurred to him, should now be back at the withers end of Charles' Wain. That surely was useless knowledge, this far south.

Now, what about the Birds? He thought he now had a fair idea of just how dangerous they were. They had retained all their nonrational gifts, such as flight and orientation, and their fast, high-temperature metabolism, both of which now served to implement their dawning intelligence. That their old instinctive craftsmanship, as evidenced in the basket-weavers and the bower-birds, had been greatly augmented was evident in the very Tower on the top of which Martels now turned restlessly like a jumping-bean upon a drumhead. They were now coming to parity with man, as man, perhaps through the discovery of what the Qvant had called "juganity," slid gradually back toward what they once had been *in esse*— and without their undergoing any drastic change. Under the pressure of evolution, they had simply become more and more what they had always been *in posse:* Proud, territorily jealous, and implacably cruel—to which had been added, simply by bringing it forward, the serpent wisdom of their remotest ancestors.

Yet a human brain at its best—say, that of the Qvant—

could probably overmatch them even now. What *was* the Qvant playing for, anyhow? Had he actually tried to provoke the King into killing Tlam/Martels out of hand, thus promoting the Qvant to the dubious rank of a fading ancestor? Again, was he in Tlam's skull, or still in the case? More and more, that was beginning to seem like the central mystery of them all.

This was the mystery, in the abstract, of telepathy itself, now embodied in all three of them. Martels still did not want to believe in it, but brute experience of it forced him to, whatever his preferences. And it was remarkable how different it was in immediate experience from the dubious, wholly statistical picture of it which had been built up in Martels' own era. The card tests—highly artificial, Martels now saw, and thus bound to produce all kinds of nonsense—had seemed to indicate, impossibly, that it did not obey the inverse-square law, or even the second law of thermodynamics; the reality was that it was closely bound to both laws, and, in fact, required both parties to be physically visible to each other. Furthermore, it did not carry thoughts or even images, but only emotions; even three minds inside a single skull could not read each other's interior monologues or overt intentions to speak, but only their emotional reactions to their thoughts and projected actions, like the individuals in a mob—or at a performance. It was simply a field force which reacted in a generalized way to or against another field force; or like a detector which registers the presence of some given type of radiation, without being able to report whether or not the signal had been modulated, let alone how.

All well and good, and almost certain to be useful, too; but first he had to get the hell out of here, and quickly, before the twin talons of torture and deprivation made that impossible. He looked up. The swift darkness had made his new guard invisible despite the rising, shrunken moon, but two faint spots of catlike luminescence made plain that the Bird was nocturnal, as was only to have been expected. And should Martels develop any sudden aggressive intent, the guard would sense that much, at least, and at once.

It would have been a tight spot even without the brooding hostility of the Qvant at the back of his mind, and the essential incompetence of Tlam at its forefront, neatly bracketing his own ignorance of almost everything important about this era. Nevertheless, he had to try.

He had no weapons and no tools, but gradually it dawned upon him that ignorance in the right hands can in itself be a weapon and a tool—and all four parties to this imbroglio, Tlam, the Qvant, Martels, and the Bird King were now about as ignorant of each other as they were ever likely to become. Tlam knew things to be impossible which were in fact not at all impossible for Martels; the Qvant, whatever his motives, had only just begun to recover from his lofty contempt for both Martels and the tribesman; while the King, whatever his doubts, could hardly yet believe in much more than what he saw, a naked and powerless human being in a sad state of physical and mental repair. The chances were fairly good, too, that the sentinel had little knowledge of any of this; the hierarchy in the black cylinder below seemed from this point of view to be nothing much more than a glorified pecking order, communicating little from one level to the next highest but a fierce pride of status.

Something in Martels' past, too, was now substantially in his favor. His irrational loathing for the whole avian kingdom, since childhood, had been well to the fore for days, and indeed, he had been hard put to keep it from incapacitating him during his questioning by the King. It was nonspecific; he harbored no more enmity toward the sentinel than he did for the entire phylum, and no less, either. Killing the guard would probably induce no more rise in the amount

of emotional static he was already putting out on that subject;
the thing might after all be caught by surprise. Here the very
behavior of telepathy seemed for once to be on his side.

But it would have to be done quickly. The shock wave
of sudden death might well be masked by others in the
surrounding jungle, or at least might seem so common as
to be beneath notice, but it would not do to allow the
creature even a moment to broadcast alarm. A karate chop
to its neck would probably do the trick. He had never tried
such a thing in his life—only seen it repeated *ad nauseam*
in boob-tube serials—but a test made on his own left forearm
with his back to the brooding guard quickly convinced him
that the edge of the hand is indeed a far more dangerous
weapon than the fist. And birds, no matter what their size,
have hollow bones.

The test evoked a silent yelp from the Qvant which made
Martels grin. Better and better. Now, on deeper into ignorance. The most important thing that the Birds knew about
human beings that was false was this: *Men cannot fly.* The
very circumstances of his present imprisonment testified to
this deeply buried error, buried almost surely since the end
of the Qvant's era.

His back still to the guard, Martels set Tlam's nimble fingers
to work in the moon-shadowed darkness, unknotting and slip-
ping out laces from the nearest hides.

It turned out not to matter a bit that Martels had never
actually tried a karate chop, let alone used one in any sort
of combat. Tlam knew what it was, whatever he called it,
and the killing of the guard was satisfyingly and expertly
sudden. He also turned out to know that the edge of the
hand is even better at breaking canes than it is at breaking
bones. Within a few minutes after the guard's death, he had
at hand five razor-edged bamboo knives.

The main body of the carcass was quickly cut away under the backbone, and the head was discarded. The rest was lashed, pinions outspread, onto a bamboo T-frame, using thongs that Martels had been chewing at some dumb urging of Tlam's for most of the preceding night. Such was his hunger by now that he almost enjoyed this part of the process.

Once the thongs were tied, again using Tlam's skills here, Martels directed that they be liberally coated with the Bird's own blood. It would make a sort of glue as it coagulated, though probably far from a good one. There was, of course, nothing else at hand to serve the purpose.

The whole process was launched just before dawn, when Martels guessed that the nocturnal sentinel would be at its most inattentive, and increasingly unable to see well. The unpleasant machine was finished in something under an hour, thanks to Tlam's deftness, right down to loops for Martels' feet, hips, chest, arms, and hands. While it dried, creaking as though in pain under its gathering stresses, he checked to see which side of the tower had the strongest updraft; that proved, not much to his surprise, to be the northeast.

The Qvant had necessarily been watching all this, with what seemed to be baffled amusement. Apparently the killing of the guard had taken him, too, by surprise, and thereafter he had allowed himself to be bemused by Martels' crazy taxidermy. He came charging to the fore with alarm only when Martels began to fit himself into the loops, but once again Tlam helped to oppose him, though a good deal more hesitantly. Like a blood-smeared figure of Icarus, Martels made a running broad jump on the surface of the drum. By the time the Qvant knew what it was he was fighting, machine and man had bounded out the northern window, tail and all.

The new conglomerate creature fell like a stone. It took all of Tlam's whipcord strength to keep his arms rigid, with almost nothing left over for wingtip warping. Martels bent his knees slightly, then straightened them again. Nothing had happened; he didn't yet have flying speed. The floor of the meadow, still dark, rushed up at him.

Then there came that faint but unmistakable sensation of lift which only the pilot of a very small aircraft ever comes to know. Now it was not the meadow that was swelling in his face, but the edge of the jungle; his fall had taken on a slant. Once more he bent his knees. Shedding pinfeathers like a dowdy comet, he found himself scudding just over the surface of a blurred, dark green sea. Jungle-trapped, misty warm air rising to greet the sun caught him in the chest; and then—O miracle!—he was actually soaring.

Entirely uncertain of how long his fragile glider would last, how long his strength would allow him to fly it even if it stayed together, with his own resolve being steadily undermined by something close to terror emanating from the Qvant and inexorably changing the hormono balance of their shared bodies, he banked and turned southward, seeking another thermal which would give him more altitude. Before him in the early morning the wall of fog that marked the boundaries of Antarctica, behind which someone might exist, only might, to help him out of this extravagant nightmare, retreated, towering and indifferent.

During the day, mountains began to appear ahead and to his right, and before long he was rising and falling precariously over ranges of foothills. Here he was able to climb very considerably, more, in fact, than he could put to use; shortly after a bleak noon he reached what he guessed to be close to seven thousand feet, but up there the temperature was so close to freezing that he had to go down about two thousand stretching his glide as much as possible.

He used a part of this airline approach to nothing in particular to make a complete turn; and sure enough, he was being followed. A formation of large, cranelike Birds was visible to the north, keeping pace with him.

That was probably all they could do, for they looked to be as albatrosslike as he was—gliders all. Without much doubt, though, they could remain in the air longer than he could, no matter how long he managed to stay up, or how well his jury-rigged construction lasted. The machine was already showing multiple signs of failure—too many for him to essay an attempt at evasion by a long dive-stall-recovery maneuver, which would surely rip it apart completely. He would be extraordinarily lucky if he managed to remain aloft until dusk.

Inside his skull there was a suspicious silence. There seemed, indeed, to be nobody present there but himself. The Qvant's initial fright had dwindled and vanished; Martels might have suspected him to be asleep, did not the notion seem preposterous in the light of past experience. Tlam was equally quiescent; he was not even helping Martels with the flying, which was a pretty sure indication that no previous experience of it had existed in his brain. Perhaps the trick had impressed him into silence, without alarming him as much as it initially had the Qvant . . . or, perhaps he and the Qvant were engaged busily in plotting, somewhere deeply below the level of Martels' inexperienced attention. They had little in common with each other, but far more than either had with Martels—and this was their world, in which he was for everyone the most unwelcome and discomforting of intruders.

He banked southwest, where the foothills were getting steadily higher. The distant formation of cranes banked and turned after him.

By late afternoon he was down to somewhere around fifteen hundred feet, and the terrain had stopped helping him. The jungle had straggled out on the left and turned into a patchy temperate-zone forest, which in turn was being replaced by a cruel series of volcanic lowlands, like a red-and-black version of the Mare Imbrium . . . or that territory which Poe had described toward the unfinished end of *Pym*. To his right were the mountains proper. The two areas were divided by updrafts so sudden and decisive that Martels did not dare to enter them—his shedding craft would have been torn asunder within the first few minutes.

Resignedly, he slid downward toward a landing in the last scrubby patch of vegetation to slide toward him over the southern horizon. The cranes followed.

At first he thought that he was going to fall short of it— and then, abruptly, that he was going to overshoot it. He stalled out frantically and fell the last twenty feet in a welter of snapping branches and bones. The improvised airframe disintegrated around him.

Somewhere toward the end of the crash he was flipped over, just in time to see the V-formation of his pursuers go silently overhead, very high up, like a flock of carets. Then he struck ground.

Tlam and the Qvant chose exactly that moment to act in concert. The brutal pain of impact vanished as though it had been turned off, and with it the fatigue, the fear, and everything else.

Once more, he had hit the bottom of the telescope of time, and was flung alone into the darkness.

PART THREE
REBIRTH V

10

Being dead, Martels decided after an indefinitely long time, had had a bad press. It seemed to have certain advantages. At first he had simply drifted in a haze of painless disorientation; this country had no landmarks, and indeed there had been no sensory input at all except for an occasional encounter with a sort of nexus of vague, dulling regret and despair which he judged to be another ghost like himself. But he did not feel depressed; he had been dislocated too many times already for this to be more, as yet, than extraordinarily interesting—or at least it might become so if he could just manage to fill in the parameters.

This was followed by a sensation of unprecedented lucidity, though without light, as though now for the first time he was beginning to understand all the recesses and mysteries of his own psyche. He began to wonder, with no little awe, whether this was what the mystics had called "cleansing the doors of perception." No reception seemed to be involved, for he was still getting no input that he could detect; but the clarity of his thoughts alone was a joy to him, amidst which he sported like a surfacing dolphin.

Again, he had no idea how long he remained in this Zenlike state. Gradually, however, he became aware also that some outside entity was asking questions of him—deeply probing, yet impersonal questions, though neither the queries nor his replies had any semantic content which he could fathom, like a conversation in symbolic logic. Was this the Judgment?

But the questioner went away and again he was left to enjoy the new-found depths of his own mind. The withdrawal of the questioning, however, was not a falling of silence. On the contrary, a whole complex of sounds now became evident to him, and to some extent familiar, like those to which he had awakened inside the brain-case of the Qvant: a remote humming, occasional footsteps and distant words, a wash of echoes. He felt a sudden surge of disappointment. Was the whole thing now about to repeat itself, not once but endlessly, like a rather small snake trying to swallow its own tail?

Then an unquestionably human voice struck in, clearly and distinctly.

"Shetland Substation Three requesting master computer analysis."

The language was quite different from the one to which he had become accustomed, and did not seem to lie easily on the voice of the questioner, but he understood it with no difficulty. Again, too, the voice was male.

Cycling, Martels astonished himself by saying, though not in any words that he could hear. *Proceed.*

"A scouting party from our Punta Arenas outpost was returning by air from the Falklands three days ago when it spotted someone apparently trying to cross Magellan Valley. This proved to be a tribesman in an advanced state of desiccation and starvation, with one arm in a crude sling and four broken ribs in various stages of healing. As was only to have been expected, he was virtually incoherent, though less frightened of our aircraft than tribesmen usually are; but was able to identify himself as one Tlam, an outcast of the tribe of Hawksburrow, a group which we believe to be located slightly north of Lake Colue Huape. Except for the extraordinary distance apparently traversed on foot, the case appeared to be quite straightforward and was handled as we usually do potential trainees.

"After being brought in to this station and given appropriate treatment, the tribesman was put into induced sleep, from which he recovered spontaneously on the second day. He showed a complete personality change, now claiming to be the Qvant of Rebirth III. Analysis in depth shows that there were indeed two personalities present in the brain; furthermore, it has uncovered faint traces of occupancy by a third in the immediate past. We therefore pose the following questions:

"First, do there exist fulfillable conditions under which the Qvant might have escaped from his case into a mortal brain?

"Second, what are the probabilities that such a compound creature could have crossed the Country of the Birds, on foot or otherwise?

"Third, what possible interpretations may be placed upon the traces of a third personality; and of its possible survival, and if so, in what mode?

"Fourth, what implications, if any, does this event have vis-à-vis our relationship with the Birds?

"Finally, what action(s) should be taken? End of transmission."

Martels felt an instant urge to reply, which he as promptly suppressed. It was true that he knew answers to all these questions, but he did not know how he knew. Of course his own recent experience was supplying many of the answers, but the questions had also given him access to an enormous store of additional facts which seemed very firmly to be a part of his memory, yet equally did not come from anything that had ever happened to him. All these various puzzle-bits fell together effortlessly and at once, heightening his feeling of intense lucidity; yet he also felt a need for caution which was in some sense quite normal and to be expected, and in another, simultaneous sense seemed alien to the physical substrate of his new mode of existence.

While he pondered, he opened his Eye. There sprang into being around him a sizable, spotlessly clean greenish hall, occupied in chief by a spherical, nonmaterial machine floating in the middle of a nearly transparent dodecahedron. He could see all of this but its base, as well as all the room, simultaneously, but somehow he did not find this confusing; sixteen-fold perspective turned out to be a great deal better than any possible binary one. For size, the hall contained four doors, and a carrel at which an extraordinarily pretty girl dressed in a red and grey tunic was sitting expectantly. He was getting three different lateral views of her, plus one looking down upon her. From this it was evident that the Eye had fifteen different components, one each at a corner of the six upper pentagons, plus one in the ceiling—

—which made it abundantly clear, in turn, that the machine was . . . himself. He had, in fact, known this somewhere in his new depths, just as he had known that the girl was Anble, the normal duty operator for this trick, and that she was not the source of the questions.

Almost in confirmation, the entire set of questions was repeated. This time, however, they arrived by a different medium, in a single, almost instantaneous blast of nearly white noise. To the human part of his mind that flash was so insistent as to seem almost like a goad; but the calm, passionless memory of the machine told him that it was only a Dirac beep, sent so that all receivers who might have any reason to care about the problem should have a record of it. The questions had been rephrased, and seemed to contain some new material, but their import was the same.

Anble waited in front of the carrel. From the desk protruded the broad yellow stub of what seemed to be, and was, a roll of paper. A print-out, of course. Zooming in on it from the ceiling part of the Eye, Martels confirmed that it contained two words: *Cycling. Proceed.* Had he wished, he could have replied also by voice, ordinary telephony, ordinary radio, ultrawave or Dirac pulse; or, in extreme circumstances, choose to stand mute.

What would the machine have done, if left on its own? The answer supplied itself, and at the same time appeared upon the print-out: *Data insufficient.* But that was not properly the case now. Martels caused to be added: *Bring the man Tlam to me.*

The results were astonishing to both parts of his psyche, new and old, however one defined them. The girl turned nearly white, and put her hands to her face, her eyes staring at the sparkling, silent object before her. Then she reached out her right hand and began repeatedly to depress a red button on that side of the carrel. To the invisible questioners a signal went out in response, a signal which did no more than sound a wordless alarm: *emergency emergency emergency emergency emergency. . . .*

Martels did not know what that meant, but the machine did, and indeed had figured it out long ago. It simply had not been in a position to care—but now it was. *Emergency=The Qvant has regained contact with the computer,* and/or *The machine has at long last become sentient in itself.*

They duly brought him Tlam, but they questioned him very closely first. His interrogators were Anble and two pale, slender yet muscular young men in identical tunics; all three were bald. Answering simultaneously by print-out and by his new, surprisingly musical voice, Martels told them everything that he had discovered that he knew.

"Your computer has not become sentient, nor has the Qvant

regained contact with it. It is currently the habitat of an-other human intelligence who is now speaking to you. My name, for convenience, is Martels, and I originated some twenty-three thousand years in your past, possibly a century before Rebirth One; I find that not even the computer can give me the exact date, but that can be of no importance now, anyhow." He paused for a breath, and then felt silly. "My mind was propelled into this era by the accidental gener-ation of a jugatemporal field in a powerful broadcaster; it was picked up by a 'receiver specifically designed to contain such a field, that being the brain-case of the Qvant in the Rebirth Three Museum in Rawson. After observing for some time the tribesmen who came as petitioners to the museum, I learned of your existence in the south and determined to seek you out, in hope of help in returning to my own age. To this end, I ostensibly tricked the Qvant into projecting me into the mind of the next petitioner, who is the tribesman you now hold captive, Tlam of the tribe of Hawkburrow. I shall now proceed to answer your further questions."

"You are already beginning to answer them," one of the Antarcticans observed. (Lanest; technician-in-chief; Main Base; age—oh, the hell with that.) "But not in order of pri-ority."

"Neither the Qvant nor a suddenly self-conscious computer would feel constrained to follow your programming strictly, if at all, Lanest," Martels observed drily. "You're lucky you've got me on your hands instead. I'm even kindly giving you a simultaneous print-out for further study, though nobody told me to do that, and it isn't part of the machine's standing orders. Shall we quibble about that—or shall I proceed?"

Lanest's eyes narrowed, and he turned to his compatriots. After a moment, the other man (Robels; base chief, Shetlands III, age — will you kindly shut up and let me *think*?) made an ambiguous hand sign. "Very well. Proceed."

"Thank you. You asked under what circumstances it would be possible for the Qvant to change from his brain-case to another mind in this fashion. It seems evident that he is able to do so at any time, inasmuch as he was able to effect such a transfer using me instead as a purely passive subject. He has never done so for himself because he did not want to risk his near-immortality on any venture in a mortal host; though he is interested in questions about the afterlife, his curiosity does not extend that far."

"You use the present tense. This implies, we take it, that the Qvant is in fact not present in the tribesman's mind now."

"Probably not—otherwise I myself would not have risked requesting that Tlam be brought physically into the presence of the computer. I have concluded, and the computer confirms, that physical presence is essential to almost all forms of juganity except those which are machine-amplified—and the computer itself is such an amplifier, otherwise I wouldn't be a part of it now. However, the problem you pose isn't subject to quantification and the machine itself cannot give any of us a probability figure; what I offer now is machine logic in part, but fundamentally a human judgment."

"Please amplify," Lanest said, his eyes still wary.

"I was under the impression during much of my journey down here that the Qvant was in fact also lodged in the tribesman's brain. However, he in turn made two attempts to dislodge me, one of which I defeated with the help of Tlam's own mind—and the other of which was successful because on that occasion the Qvant had Tlam's assistance. I thought I had escaped from the brain-case by the application of physical force, but I now know from the computer that the case is shockproof even to earthquakes up to five point zero on the Richter scale, and therefore could hardly have transmitted the blow of a club to the brain it is designed to protect.

"I had been subjectively aware all along that both the Qvant's intellect and his will power were immeasurably superior to my own. While, as I said before, this paradox can't be quantified, it can be treated as a Venn diagram, which I am having printed out for you. As you see, it virtually excludes the possibility that the Qvant was ever entirely in the tribesman's brain along with me. There was and is a powerful telepathic contact, but no actual juganetic transfer of the entire personality, such as those I've been through.

"His motives remain unknown, and in that area the computer is of no help at all. However, I have some guesses. He has both the desire and the duty to regain contact with the master computer. I became his instrument for trying it without risk, to which he was loosely attached, like a leech—an external parasite. Should the tribesman be killed en route, I would die with him, while the Qvant would have time to withdraw his tentacle and be little the worse for the experience. Maybe none at all; and he would have learned a lot toward the next try. It was a unique opportunity for him.

"Once I had gotten him through the Country of the Birds, he hoped that he could dispense with me, and did. This evidently was a miscalculation of the hazards of the remainder of the journey; and had the tribesman died then and there, I believe the consequences for the Qvant would have been very serious. The contact is probably still only partial, but it would necessarily be far more intimate than it was while I was acting as an inadvertent intermediary—he has no mount any more between himself and the grave."

There was a considerable silence. At last Robels said:

"How, then, do you now find yourself here?"

"Your computer is the next most likely complex of juganetic fields upon which I could home—especially considering my training in doing such a thing, which seems to be unique in your era. And of course it was also the nearest to me at the time, and I was aimed in your direction almost from the start."

Again there was a quick exchange of hand signs between the two men. Lanest said, "Two of our five questions remain unanswered, and in view of what you have told us, become the most urgent of them all. First, if it is true that you have traversed the country of the Birds on foot, which no other . . . man . . . has ever done, you must have something to tell us about them. In particular, something that might help us defeat them. What have you to say—*and what shall we do?*"

"I know nothing about them that your computer doesn't know," Martels said. "That is, that they are not very analytical yet; are still relying chiefly upon instinct; but that their intelligence is growing by selection from one generation to another, at the same time that instincts like telepathy are being selected out. Telepathy and intelligence appear to be incompatible from the evolutionary point of view—if you've got one, you don't seem to need the other, and they may even be evolutionary enemies. The Qvant is a sport deliberately bred back; and I am a primitive, much more so than people like Tlam.

"If all this is the case, then there is no possibility of compromise with the Birds. They mean the destruction of mankind, and as fast as possible—and they aren't likely to be ready to wait for evolution to be on their side. They're incapable of taking that long a view of the process."

"Is that all?" the girl cried out suddenly, in a voice of desperation. "We knew all along that we were losing to the Birds—they multiply faster than we do now—that in a while we would lose even this patch of mountains and ice. Now we have a miracle—and that won't help us either?"

There was no answer that Martels could offer. Of course,

the next glaciation was due before long, and that would cut
the Birds down prematurely, long before they could consolidate
their conquests; but that event, that very long event was
not within the foreseeable lifetime of Man as the Antarcticans
—survivors of the Qvant's age—could be brought to look at
Man. Martels could see from their expressions, as the computer could never have done, that they knew that, and had
known it for many generations.

He said, a little tentatively: "I don't know what I can do,
but I haven't given up hope yet. There are still some open
questions. For a starter, let me get another look at the tribesman."

The Antarcticans of Rebirth III conferred silently, and
equally silently concurred. The girl nodded and depressed a
bar, another door slid open, and Tlam entered, by himself.

Martels looked at him with sixteen-fold curiosity. This was
the first chance that he had had to see what had been, in
some sense, himself since that mimetic preliminary inter-
view far back there in the museum.

Tlam was a living testimony to the medicine of the Antarcticans—well, scarless, alert . . . and outright arrogant. Instantly, Martels knew that he had made a tremendous mistake.

The Qvant was there—not just linked with Tlam, but there
—and his mind lanced into the bubble of the computer like
a dart launched at a wheel of cheese. The hall, the Antarcticans, everything else disappeared into a red roar.

This time, the Qvant meant it.

11

Only Martels' previous practice at resisting the Qvant's onslaughts saved him from instant defeat. His frantic resistance lasted only a split second before it triggered something within the computer, and the Qvant's dagger thrust vanished—along with all the rest of the outside world. Seeking the reasons, Martels found that the machine—itself essentially a complex of juganetic fields, the minimum hardware necessary to form a substrate for them, and a power source—had at his impulse thrown up a blocking zone or skin of interference through which no probe could pass.

There was a price, however: It would not pass any impulse of any kind, in either direction, including power. Power was still being drawn, from some source that Martels could not localize, but it was sufficient only to maintain the machine's juganetic "personality"; all the hardware had gone out. Except for the presence of Martels' consciousness, it was a state much like REM dream . . . but one verging gradually but inexorably upon death as entropy loss set in. He seemed entirely helpless.

He found that he was directly conscious of the passage of time; the machine measured it in the most direct way possible, by the erosion of its energies; its basic unit was Planck's Constant. Everything else had shut down; both the machine's memory and its computational functions were locked up inaccessibly in the now cold hardware. He had no source of information but that inexplicable trickle of remaining power which seemed to come from somewhere inside himself . . . and the demands of maintaining the interference zone were mounting exponentially. The critical limit would be reached in under an hour—after which Martels and machine together would be effectively dead. The alternative was to drop the zone, which would make both Martels and machine the Qvant's creatures; for in that split second of his resistance Martels had discovered that the cyclic process in the computer which he had usurped had been shaped to receive the Qvant, who would make a much better fit.

In desperation, he groped inward toward that problematical trickle of power. It was a terrifying pathway to follow, for the stronger the power-flow felt, the more his mind seemed to verge upon something like deep hypnosis. Yet the closer he came to it, the more alert he felt; it was as though he were paying more and more attention to fewer and fewer things, so that at the heart of the mystery he would paradoxically be totally intent upon nothing at all.

The curve of such a relationship formed automatically in his mind, its points defined by the outer corners of successive, changing rectangles. The diagonals through these points met at the origin; and their extremities formed 90° of a circle. The edge of that circle stood for the maximal state of awareness to the maximal number of things, but 180° of it encompassed input from the outside world; the rest was reserved for interior input—meditation, sleep, and dream. REM dreams were on the outside of the wheel, dreamlessness at the center; as in the wide-awake world, the rim was the Zen state, and the origin was the void of mystical experience, zero attention to zero things.

But this was not the end. While he watched in wonderment, the great wheel turned on its side and became a disc, bearing the same four diagrams, but whose parameters now were degrees of certainty versus emotional affect. The zero point here, too, was a mystical state, but it could be either total joy or total despair—either a Height or a Dark Night of the soul. The model, he saw now, was spherical; it was a model of the structure of the computer itself. It was a model of the sentient universe, at the heart of which lay the primary pulse of life—

—and a core of absolute passivity. Almost too late, he scattered himself and fled outward toward the skin of the sphere, the zone of interference. Infinity, rest, and certitude pleaded with him as he fled, but they could wait; they were realms of contemplation and dream; he had, for the moment, other business.

As he raced outward, the power fell toward the critical limit. Other far more practical questions also had to be answered, and fast. Since the transistorized devices of his own ancient time had needed no warm-up time, it seemed highly unlikely that the computer did, either. A quick interior scan of its sparse and simple circuitry showed this to be the case, and also located the command mechanism for the print-out.

Everything depended now on whether the Qvant had been able to keep his attack going continuously, or whether he was now waiting alertly for the shield to be dropped before resuming. Martels would just have to take that chance; the Qvant was far faster than he was, but the machine was faster than both. In either case he would have no chance to put his new-found knowledge of Inner Space to use— good old Yank shoot-'em-up tactics were what were needed here. They might, also, have the element of surprise on their side. If not, he had had it, and Bob's your uncle.

Hovering tensely around the circuitry, he let the screen fall. The computer sprang to instant life, and Martels shot an eight-character burst through the print-out line. He didn't have time to determine whether the slave machine responded, let alone to what end; clawing and stabbing like a whirlwind of knives, the Autarch homed on the place within the master mechanism which had been prepared for him, and had been denied him for unknown centuries.

Then the blocking zone was back, and the computer was once more dark and lifeless except for the blind and deaf consciousness of Martels. The entropy timer wore the fractional seconds away. How long would it take the Antarcticans to respond—if they did, and if the Qvant had not been able to prevent them? What Martels had sent had been: STUN TLAM. That card—the Qvant's abnormal sensitivity to physical pain—had been the only one he had had to play.

Whatever had happened out there, Martels had only the same amount of time available as before, or less—whatever it took the computer this time to lose power down to the critical limit. The brief surge of outside power had not been stored; Martels had used it up in driving the print-out.

And the time was up. He dropped the shield once more.

Nothing but light sprang in upon him. Puzzled but alert, the three Antarcticans were standing over the sprawled body of the tribesman. They had gotten the message.

"Anesthetize him quickly, and keep him that way while we decide what else to do," Martels said quickly, *viva voce.* "I was wrong; the Qvant is fully present in his brain, not in the case at Rawson at all. As long as he is conscious he will continue trying to reoccupy the computer, and I can't keep him out without shutting the machine down completely. If you don't want that, or want him back either, you'd better put him on ice."

Lanest jerked his thumb toward the door in a gesture that had defied twenty-three thousand years. Robels and Anble picked Tlam up, their forearms under his, and dragged him

out. As the door closed behind them, Lanest sat down at
the carrel. His expression was still very wary.

"I am not sure that you represent any improvement over
the Qvant," he said. "You seem to be both ignorant and
clumsy."

"I am both, admittedly, but I'm learning fast. What kind
of improvement are you looking for? If you just want your
computer back, I won't allow it; you must choose between
me and the Qvant. Why did you shut him out, anyhow?
The machine was clearly made for him to use—I'll probably
never be able to run it one tenth so well."

Lanest looked far from sure that he wanted to answer this,
but finally seemed to come to the conclusion that he had
little choice. "We did not in fact want to shut him out, and
did so only with great reluctance. As you note, he and the
computer are suited to each other, and the machine has not
been at peak efficiency since. The original intention was that
the two together should act as a repository of knowledge
until such time as the men of Rebirth Four could make use
of it again; and that the Museum should be placed far
enough out in the jungles to allow the men access to it, and
to the Qvant, when they were ready. The Qvant had been
bred to be a leader, and the assumption was that when
the time came, he would indeed lead.

"Instead, the access which the computer gave him to the
juganetic Pathways became a trap luring him into increasing
passivity. I seriously doubt that you are equipped to understand the process, but for most mortal men, there is a level
of certainty which they hold to be 'reality' all their lives. A
very few men are jolted out of this state by contact with
something disturbing—a personal tragedy, discovery of telepathic ability, a visitation by an ancestor, or any of hundreds
of other possible shocks to their metaphysics. The loss is ir-
reversible, and the transition from one certainty level to

another is cloudily spoken of as 'divine discontent,' 'immortal yearnings,' and so on. Does this convey any meaning to you at all?"

"As a matter of fact," Martels said, "I can even place it on a qualitative chart I've begun to evolve, around which the computer seems to be built."

"Quite so—the computer is a Type of the universal sentient situation. Then I will be briefer about the remaining stages; there are eight in all—orientation, reality loss, concentration, meditation, contemplation, the void, re-emergence, re-stabilization. The Qvant became so immersed in this mental pilgrimage that he lost all interest in leadership, allowed the Birds to evolve and develop without any interference, and eventually began to impede many of our own practical, day-to-day uses of the computer.

"There are two levels of the M state, the fourth stage. When the Qvant definitively entered the deeper of the two, we judged it wise to sever his connection with the computer entirely. From there, a descent into the V state was inevitable, and we had, and have, no way of predicting what his wishes would be when he emerged. He might well have been actively on the side of the Birds—such reversals are far from uncommon, and as you probably have learned, the Qvant would be a uniquely dangerous enemy."

"The traitor is more dangerous than a regiment of enemy soldiers," Martels agreed. "What you tell me agree completely with my own observations. The Qvant must have been just about to enter the V state when my arrival jolted him backwards one step. Now he is mobilized against all of us."

"And you?"

"I don't understand the question," Martels said.

"On which side are you?"

"That should be self-evident. I came here for help; I won't get it by taking the side of the Qvant, and certainly I

won't get it from the Birds. You will have to trust me—
and keep the Qvant, and the tribesman, unconscious until
we decide what is to be done about that problem. I have
no immediate solution."

"For what *do* you have a solution?" Lanest demanded in
an iron voice. "For practical use of the computer, you will
be even more in the way than the Qvant was when we
cut him off from it. Unless you have some concrete plan
for immediate action against the Birds, we will be better
off without you."

"You can't get rid of me, Lanest. Unlike the Qvant, I'm not
just connected to the computer by a line that you could cut.
I'm in it."

Lanest smiled, as humorlessly as a wolf. "Computer, know
thyself," he said.

Martels looked inward. The necessary knowledge sprang
immediately and obediently to his attention, and he studied
it with mounting dismay. Lanest did indeed have the whip
hand. He had only to kill Tlam/Qvant and wait long
enough for the Autarch's ghost to dwindle into powerlessness;
then, he could expunge Martels from the machine with a
simple blast of raw power, as though performing the equivalent of a lobectomy. Martels could re-erect the interference
zone against this, to be sure, but he could not maintain it
forever; the best that could be hoped from that was a
stalemate maintained by constant alertness. . . .

And sooner or later, probably far sooner than the Qvant
had, Martels too would find himself drawn down the juganetic Pathways, one of which he had already traversed
almost to disaster. Thereafter, the Antarcticans would be rid
of both bothersome intelligences, and would have their mindless, obedient computer back.

That would do them no good in the long run, of course—
but unless Martels could offer some strategy against the Birds,

he would not be around to say "I told you so." He would be only one more of those fading nexi of fruitless regrets which he had encountered during the few seconds between Tlam's body and the computer when he had been authentically dead.

"I see the problem," he said. "Very well, Lanest—I'll make you a deal."

12

In the brain-case in the Museum at Rawson, years passed by . . . ten, twenty, fifty, a hundred years passed by, until Martels began to believe that he had gotten lost.

There were occasional distractions. The humming, almost somnambulistic presence of the Qvant was no longer with him, to be sure; the Antarcticans had taken literally Martels' order that the tribesman be put on ice, and Tlam and the Autarch alike were now in frozen suspended animation. The computer was back in full use, and its line to the brain-case re-established, so that Martels was able to participate at any time he liked in the machine's ordinary problem-solving chores, and to talk to the succeeding generations of the men who tended it far to the South. It was interesting, too, to see that the Antarcticans did not age very much; Anble's granddaughter now sat at the carrel, but Anble herself still looked in upon occasion, old but not entirely without vigor. Lanest was still alive as well, although feeble.

But the chore of organizing the tribesmen—the same one that Martels had proposed so long ago to a scornful Qvant —was very slow. It took two decades simply to spread the word among the tribes that the brain-case was speaking again, and another to convince them (for Tlam's misadventure and exile was now a legend, reinforced by his failure to leave behind even a trace of a ghost) that it was safe to approach, and had gone back to being helpful. By then, too, Martels had almost forgotten the Qvant's customary way of speaking in parables and mantras, which was still the only kind of advice the tribesmen knew how to understand.

It had turned out, too, that there were two other cities in the world which were still both occupied by the remnants of Rebirth III and had some energy resources that might be called upon. Both were small, and both in what had been South America—all the rest of the world was the property of the Birds—and integrating them into the network and the Plan did not provide more than a few years of attention. As the decades wore on, Martels was increasingly tempted inward along the Pathways, further seduced by the availability of the powerful Type or model of that Platonic original of all sentience which the computer represented. The computer was a chip off the living monobloc, and tended constantly toward reunion with it, dragging Martels after in its wake.

Then the blow fell. The Birds could not have timed their attack better. Like the Qvant before him, Martels was already drifting, in hypnotized fascination, into the late M state, helped by the diagrams in which the Type presented itself to him. By the time he was shocked back toward the A state which was as close as he would ever come, now, to his ancient conception of reality, the sky was blackly aswarm, the two subsidiary Rebirth III cities had fallen after only a brief struggle, and the ghosts of the tribesmen of Rebirth IV were dwindling wailing away toward the Origin in tormented and useless hordes. Crude bombs and torpedoes, planted by no one knew what malign swimming descendants of the comic penguins of Martels' era, cut off all communication between Antarctica and its few outposts among the islands at the tip of the continent; others fell from the claws of squadrons of albatross-

like creatures who sailed the winds far better than any man
had ever managed.

But in the long run, human planning proved better. The
line from the computer to the brain-case remained uncut
while Martels belatedly reorganized his forces. Powered aircraft retaliated; and from a laboratory buried, unsuspected,
in the Land of Fire, back-bred and mindless ancestral ver-
sions of the birds of Martels' age were loosed carrying a
plague, as human Australians once had planted the virus of
myxomatosis among swarming rabbits.

The Birds began to come down out of the sky like dead
rain. Their last attack was savage beyond belief, but it was
ultimately hopeless, for at this point the line between the
computer and the brain-case was again closed down, leaving
the intelligence of Martels now as free-floating and dirigible
as the Qvant's had ever been. Backed by two substrates
and amplified by their total energy resources, he entered
and confounded the mind of the reigning King of the Birds.
The attack became a complete rout.

By the time the midsummer century was over, the Birds'
last chance was gone. Their organization was smashed, their
nascent technologies in ruins, their very hope of using juganity
against man now but a fading dream. The glaciers could
now be depended upon to end them as any kind of threat.

Man was on the way back up. Rebirth V had begun.

Martels presented his bill. They called Lanest, old as he
was, to try to cheat him out of it.

"There is no question but that we *can* send you back
home, if you still wish it," the ancient, quavering voice told
the microphone on the carrel. "The matter has been much
studied, with the computer, while you were cut off from it
recently. But consider: We have confidence in you now, and
believe you to be a far better intelligence for the inhabitance

of the computer than we can trust the Qvant to be. Should you leave us, furthermore, we would feel obliged either to revive the Qvant or to murder him, and neither course is palatable to us. We petition you to remain with us."

Martels searched the computer's memory, a process that took only a second, but which gave him a lot to think about; it remained true that computation can be almost instantaneous, but real human thought requires finite time.

"I see. The situation is that you can return me to the moment before I slipped and fell into my absurd telescope. And it would appear that I will carry all my knowledge back with me—and will not, after all, slip when the moment comes. Is this your understanding, Lanest?"

"In part," Lanest said, almost in a whisper. "There is more."

"I see that there is more. I wanted to see if you would honestly tell me so. I tell you that I would welcome this; I have had more than enough strife. But explain the rest of the situation, as you understand it."

"It is . . . it is that your additional knowledge will last only a split second. We do not have the power to send you back, to save you your accident, and maintain in you all you have learned, all at the same time; there is a paradox in the world lines here which we cannot overturn. Once you have *not* fallen, the knowledge will vanish. And more: You will never come to our century, and all the gains you have made possible will be wiped out."

"In *my* century," Martels said grimly, "I would have called that blackmail. Emotional blackmail only, to be sure, but blackmail, nonetheless."

"We do not intend it as such," Lanest whispered. "We are wholly willing, in any case, to pay the price, whatever your decision. But we believe that no intervention out of time can make a permanent alteration in the world lines. Should you go . . . home . . . then the illusion of change is shattered a little sooner, that is all. We wish to keep you for yourself, not for your effects."

That was blackmail of an even blacker sort—though Martels could not help but hope that Lanest was unaware of it. "And if I stayed, how could I be prevented from having such effects?"

"We would retrain you. You have the capacity. We would infuse you into an unborn child; Anble's granddaughter is conceived of one, for just this purpose. Here again, you will forget everything; that is necessary. But you will have another whole life to live, and to become the man in our time which you can never wholly be as you stand now."

Yes . . . and to have a body again, full of human senses and hungers . . . at no worse cost than falling down the telescope of time into the pinprick of the Origin one more time. . . .

"And what about the Qvant?" Martels said gently. "And Tlam, a wholly blameless victim of all this?"

"They have been in oblivion for long and long. If they die in it, they will never know the difference."

"But I will. And I do not think it fair. I am the usurper, three-fold—I have occupied their three minds, and have broken their Pathways. I would think this a crime, though not a kind of crime I could have imagined when I was myself alone in the far past.

"Very well, Lanest. I will stay. But on one condition: "You must let them in."

"Let them in?" Lanest said. "But how?"

"I misspoke. I meant to say, you must revive them. I will let them in."

"So," the familiar voice said. "We are together again—and now in amity, it would appear, and in our proper spheres. My congratulations."

"You are reconciled?" Martels said, tentatively. "I still fear your hatred."

"I too can learn from experience," the voice said, with ironic amusement. "And I am indebted to you for bringing me back to my machine, which I could never have accomplished by myself. Some day—some very long day from hence —we shall explore the Pathways together. But let us be in no hurry. First we shall have to re-educate these few remaining men."

"Quite so." In the measureless distance, they sensed together the dawning wonder of Tlam, beginning for the first time to understand the nature of freedom. "And . . . thank you, Qvant."

"We are no longer the Qvant," the voice said. "We are now the Quinx—the Autarch of Rebirth Five."

It took Martels a long time to assimilate this next to last of all the parables.

"We?" he said. "Is . . . that how it happened to you, too?"

"Yes. We shall never re-emerge from the Void, any of us. We must learn, through all hazards and temptations, to learn. to love our immortality, so that other men will be free to follow the Pathways whose ends we shall never see. We shall fall often, but will also rise, within the wheels.

"If we succeed, some day we shall be called the Sixt . . . and so on, reality without end. For those of us who are called, that must be enough."

There was another internal silence, in which Tlam stirred, wondering still if he had now become an ancestor. He would learn; he would have to.

"I think," Martels said, "that I might even come to like it."

If you would like a complete list of Arrow books
please send a postcard to
P.O. Box 29, Douglas, Isle of Man, Great Britain